Crash lan

Bruce checked the altimeter and notched in the throttle. The small plane hesitated, then the propeller bit into the thin air and lurched them higher. His handsome face was pale. "What's the matter?" Lila asked quickly.

The plane dipped. "We're on empty," Bruce said, his voice shaking. "We're going down."

"I'll call the traffic control center," Lila said, seizing the mike from the instrument panel.

Bruce shook his head. "We're too low—the mountains are interfering with the transmission!"

The stall-warning indicator began to blare. Bruce slammed his palm against the instrument panel. "Damn—we're below stall speed!" he shouted.

We're going to crash, she realized. *There's no hope.*

"I think we might make it to that ledge!" Bruce shouted.

"We can't survive a hit this hard!" She was screaming now.

Bruce swore desperately. "I can't see the ledge anymore! Damned fog!"

Lila opened her eyes. A huge wall of rock erupted before her. Lila heard her scream echo wildly around the cabin. Then blackness slammed into her.

Bantam Books in the Sweet Valley University series
Ask your bookseller for the books you have missed

#1 COLLEGE GIRLS
#2 LOVE, LIES, AND JESSICA WAKEFIELD
#3 WHAT YOUR PARENTS DON'T KNOW . . .
#4 ANYTHING FOR LOVE
#5 A MARRIED WOMAN
#6 THE LOVE OF HER LIFE
#7 GOOD-BYE TO LOVE
#8 HOME FOR CHRISTMAS
#9 SORORITY SCANDAL

Coming soon:
#10 NO MEANS NO

And don't miss
Sweet Valley University Thriller Edition #1:
WANTED FOR MURDER

Sorority Scandal

Written by
Laurie John

Created by
FRANCINE PASCAL

BANTAM BOOKS
NEW YORK • TORONTO • LONDON • SYDNEY • AUCKLAND

RL 6, age 12 and up

SORORITY SCANDAL

A Bantam Book / February 1995

Sweet Valley High® and Sweet Valley University™
are trademarks of Francine Pascal
Conceived by Francine Pascal
Produced by Daniel Weiss Associates, Inc.
33 West 17th Street
New York, NY 10011

ISBN: 0-553-56654-7

Published simultaneously in the United States and Canada

Bantam Books are published by Bantam Books, a division of Bantam Doubleday Dell Publishing Group, Inc. Its trademark, consisting of the words "Bantam Books" and the portrayal of a rooster, is Registered in U.S. Patent and Trademark Office and in other countries. Marca Registrada. Bantam Books, 1540 Broadway, New York, New York 10036.

PRINTED IN THE UNITED STATES OF AMERICA

OPM 0 9 8 7 6 5 4 3 2 1

To Jonathan David Rubin

Chapter One

"Where *are* we, Bruce?" Lila Fowler asked. "Are we still in California?" Below Bruce Patman's Cessna the snowy, jagged mountain peaks of the Sierra Nevada glittered white and rock-blue in the pale moonlight.

"Of course we are," Bruce answered over the solid drone of the propeller. "Just sit tight."

I haven't got much choice, Lila thought, swallowing hard. *Those mountains are thousands of feet down.* "Well, you've made me completely miss my sorority dinner." Fear made that comment come out even nastier than she had intended.

"Sorry," Bruce said tensely. His jaw was set.

He's scared too, Lila realized. "Turn around," she ordered.

"I can't." Bruce eased up on the throttle, and the plane dropped slightly. "I haven't got enough gas."

"At least let me fly." Lila stared down at the

mountains, gripping the instrument panel in front of her tightly with one hand. If Bruce had proved one thing in the last three hours, it was that he was a lousy pilot. Lila herself was an excellent pilot. She and her husband, Count Tisiano di Mondicci, had flown over the Alps in Italy many times.

Thinking of Tisiano, Lila felt tears fill her eyes. He had died recently in a jet-skiing accident. Maybe that was why, Lila said to herself, she was always looking for excitement these days. She couldn't brood about a dead husband when Bruce Patman was flying a plane through the snowiest mountain range in the country.

"Like *you* could get us out of this." Bruce didn't even look at her.

The mountains loomed closer.

"Jerk," Lila said angrily. She had put up with years of his being a jerk—from their days at Sweet Valley High to the moment Lila had set foot on the Sweet Valley University campus to audit classes after Tisiano had died last semester.

I'm completely at Bruce's mercy, Lila thought. *That's never happened before.* It *would* be when they were lost in the mountains in a plane without parachutes.

She checked her seat belt. It was on and pulled tight.

Near her foot Lila saw a big paper bag that her mother had packed with steak sandwiches, fruit, and high-energy trail mix. At the last minute Lila had stuffed in some gourmet chocolates.

She unwrapped a chocolate and took a bite. Might as well get some comfort.

How had she gotten into this mess? Lila wondered, chewing the slightly bitter chocolate. She should be at SVU right now, dancing in the arms of a gorgeous frat guy after the formal Theta Alpha Theta sorority dinner.

Lila looked down at her dress, an explosion of glittering dark-red spangles draped with a gauzy white evening wrap. She wore high-heeled red sandals strapped around her ankles.

The cold whistled in around the windows of the plane. It would be much colder outside—terribly, freezing cold. Lila wasn't dressed for a trip to the mountains. What if they crashed . . . ?

No. That just couldn't happen. This wasn't the movies.

"Why did I fly with you?" she muttered. "That was completely stupid. I should have frozen solid on that runway before I got in a plane with you."

Bruce gave her a brief, irritated look.

It just makes him more repulsive that he's so good-looking, Lila decided. *Like deceptive advertising or something. You can't tell that he's got a disgusting, chauvinistic personality just from his appearance.*

The plane she'd rented to fly herself back to SVU that night was in about a million pieces on the repair-shop floor. Somehow the message that she was going to rent it had gotten mixed up.

Then Bruce had appeared, whistling and jingling his keys as he swaggered to his new plane, parked at the end of one of the runways. Lila had felt an instant surge of dislike and annoyance, the way she always did when Bruce got within about thirty feet of her.

But she could either miss the Theta dinner or put up with his company for an hour. Even though she'd known it wasn't a good idea, she'd asked him for a lift.

I got a lift, all right. Lila swallowed hard. *Into the wrong mountain range. . . .*

Bruce was staring straight out the windshield. He checked the altimeter and notched in the throttle. The small plane hesitated; then the propeller bit into the thin air and lurched them higher.

His handsome face was pale. "What's the matter?" Lila asked quickly.

The plane dipped. "We're on empty," Bruce said, his voice shaking. "We're going down. Would you please help watch for a clearing? This is going to be tricky."

Lila looked down with alarm. The moon had disappeared. Boiling gray clouds of fog whirled below them. Only the tips of the mountains stood out of the clouds, like pointed teeth.

"What's your altitude?" she asked, trying to keep her voice calm.

"Ten thousand," he answered.

"Bring it up to twelve," she said. A sharp finger of rock shot out of the fog; they barely cleared it. Lila almost screamed. "These mountains are almost at ten thousand feet!" she shouted at him. "We need to be at least two thousand feet higher to clear them!" She couldn't keep the terror out of her voice.

"Don't you think I know that?" Bruce snarled. "We haven't got enough gas to go higher!"

The first wave of the fog clouds hit the plane hard. It dropped sickeningly.

"Bring it up!" Lila shouted over the whining of the strained engines and buffeting wind.

"I can't!" Bruce's voice was edged with panic too.

"I'll call the traffic-control center," Lila said, seizing the mike from the instrument panel. "We have to give them our position if we go down."

She pressed the switch on the mike. "Center, this is Cessna 140Z. Please come in. *Please*."

Bruce shook his head. "We're too low—the mountains are interfering with the transmission!"

The plane dropped farther. Lila closed her eyes. A tear coursed slowly down her cheek.

This is it, she thought. *I'm going to die in a ball of flames, just like in my dream.*

Since before Christmas, Lila had been haunted by a recurring nightmare of a plane crash. She'd thought that the dream was related to her grief over Tisiano, but now she had to wonder if she'd had a horrible premonition of her own death. *How can this happen? When I got up this morning, I didn't know today I would die. . . .*

The stall-warning indicator began to blare. Bruce slammed his palm against the instrument panel. "Damn—we're below stall speed!" he shouted.

Lila hardly heard him. *We're going to crash in about thirty seconds,* she realized. *There's no hope.*

"I think we might make it to that ledge!" he shouted.

"We'll die! We can't survive a hit this hard!" She was screaming now.

Bruce swore desperately. "I can't see the ledge anymore! Damned fog!"

Lila opened her eyes. A huge rock of solid gray granite and blowing drifts of snow erupted before her.

Lila heard her scream echo wildly around the cabin. Then blackness slammed into her.

Alison Quinn, vice president of the Theta Alpha Theta sorority, was watching Jessica Wakefield through slitted gray eyes. She set down her coffee cup and carefully wiped her mouth. "Let's get to the purpose of this brunch," she said. "I have a special announcement to make about Jessica."

Jessica felt her face pale. She sat up straighter

and stared at Alison, her blue-green eyes intense. *This is it,* she thought. *At this moment I either become a Theta or a nobody, for the rest of my days at SVU. There's no in between.*

Isabella Ricci, Jessica's close friend and former roommate, smiled at her encouragingly from across the big oak table.

Jessica tried to smile back. Nervously she pushed her golden hair behind her shoulders.

"Jessica is an impressive legacy," Alison went on. "All of us know that her mother, Alice Wakefield, was essential in making Theta Alpha Theta the number-one sorority on campus. For that reason we've decided to give Jessica another chance to become one of us. Jessica, you may repledge."

The sisters clapped. Jessica blew out her breath in a *whoosh.* They'd decided to let her live, after all.

"Congratulations, Jess," Isabella said. She walked around the table and squeezed Jessica's arm.

Jessica picked up her coffee and walked with Isabella into the spacious living room at Theta house. The sorority was an old Victorian house with high, arched ceilings, oak banisters curving up to the bedrooms on the second floor, and beautiful Persian rugs. *This is my sorority now,* Jessica thought proudly. She was so excited, it was hard to keep her face cool and dignified the way a member of an elite sorority should. "Tell me how you worked this," she said to Isabella in a low voice. "I can hardly believe Alison let me repledge. She hates me."

Isabella frowned, running a hand through her thick mane of dark hair. "She didn't want to. Alison was just outvoted by the rest of the membership."

"Great," Jessica said happily. "So most of the Thetas want me in."

"Yes, but . . ." Isabella shook her head. "I'd watch my back with Alison. She wasn't pleased, to put it mildly. You missed a lot of shouting yesterday, when we had the meeting about you. Finally Alison stalked off in a rage. That's when the rest of us voted you in."

"Alison will just have to live with the other members' decision." Jessica shrugged. "Live and let live."

"That's what I'm worried about." Isabella's warm charcoal-colored eyes were thoughtful. "Alison doesn't like losing. And she doesn't like *you*. That's a lethal combination. I wonder why you two have such a problem with each other."

"I've never had anything against Alison," Jessica protested. "She definitely started it, giving me a hard time when I was a waitress at the coffeehouse last semester."

"At least you're not doing *that* anymore." Isabella sighed.

"That, and a lot of other things," Jessica said easily. Since the Thetas were letting her repledge, obviously they were willing to forget about not only her waitressing job but also her disastrous marriage to Michael McAllery. Now the marriage was annulled. Jessica was ready for a fresh start this semester.

"Alison will get over whatever her problem is," Jessica said confidently. "I think you worry too much, Izzy."

Jessica felt eyes on her back. Turning, she saw that Alison's calculating gaze was fixed on her.

Alison started toward Jessica. The other sorority sisters, chatting in small groups in the living room, fell silent as she passed. Alison stopped in front of Jessica and stared at her.

What is wrong with her? Jessica thought. *If looks could kill, I'd be postmortem.*

"I almost forgot," Alison said, smirking. "How careless of me. You do need to do one tiny thing more to become a Theta."

"One more thing?" Jessica stared back at Alison. Alison's slate-gray eyes were so icy, it was unsettling.

"Do you think that's too much to ask?"

"No, I don't," Jessica said, tossing back her hair. *If she thinks she can psych me out, she's wrong,* she thought.

Alison smiled, but it wasn't much warmer than her glare. "Oh, I certainly hope it's no problem, or you're not going to be a Theta, after all. Not now or ever."

Jessica's heart beat faster. Just what was Alison planning?

Alison pointed a perfectly manicured finger at Jessica. "To prove your loyalty to the Thetas, Jessica, we want you to perform a challenge. Tomorrow we'll tell you exactly what that challenge is."

Just what is the witch planning? Jessica wondered, trying not to panic.

Alison smiled again. "We just want you to steal a little something for us. That's not such a big deal, is it?"

Elizabeth thumped her Romantic-poetry text on top of the rest of her books. Craning her stiff neck, she got up from her library carrel and began to wedge notebooks into her backpack.

I've done enough studying for this morning, she thought. *Three good hours. I'm back on track.*

She was completely alone in the library. Around her carrel in the first-floor stacks, no other heads were bent over assignments. Everyone else had gone out to enjoy the brilliant southern-California sunshine. Most students didn't feel any pressure to study now; the semester had just begun.

But Elizabeth had to study. Last week she had gotten the first C of her life. Unbelievably, the grade had been on an English paper. Elizabeth had been the star of every English class she had ever taken, and the grade had been a horrible shock.

"I shouldn't have tried to write a fifteen-page paper in two hours," she told herself, pushing her long blond hair back over her shoulders. "Duh."

Doing such a shoddy job on an important assignment was more like something Elizabeth's identical twin sister, Jessica, would do. Despite the fact that Elizabeth and Jessica had the same golden-blond hair, sea-green eyes, and slim, five-foot-six-inch figures, they were easy to tell apart.

Until Mike McAllery had come along, Jessica had glided from guy to guy, going through them like a bag of potato chips. Her idea of studying had been hanging out at her favorite café, taking note of who was wearing the nicest outfit. Elizabeth was more inclined toward reading poetry or working on a journalism piece. Her relationships with guys had been warm and stable—Jessica's idea of boring.

Elizabeth sighed. Her overwhelming love for Tom Watts was anything but boring. Once she'd started dating Tom, things had a mysterious way of slipping her mind—her English papers, for example.

The night before it was due, she and Tom had gone to see a really great foreign movie. At midnight she'd remembered the paper was due that day.

Professor Martin had scrawled a bright-red C

on the last page. *I expected more from you,* he had written next to it. He had asked her to meet him in his office this afternoon, probably to discuss the grade.

Elizabeth groaned. But her blue-green eyes softened at the memory of her evening with Tom. Seeing movies was part of her education, right? She and Tom were both reporters for the campus television station, WSVU. They had to stay current on popular cultural trends.

Having a love life was educational too. After the movie she and Tom had gone to his room to share a green-chili-and-pepperoni pizza. She'd never had green chili on a pizza before. Then they'd kissed passionately for hours. . . .

The nearby window blinds rustled. A tempting breeze blew through the room, sweet with the smell of mowed grass.

Behind her Elizabeth heard a soft footfall. *Creak.* She glanced over her shoulder. So someone else was studying. Or the library had mice.

Elizabeth walked around the shelves of books toward the door. "Until tomorrow," she said, directing her remark at the thick tomes. "I'll be here for at least three hours every day."

A book fell sharply to the floor behind her. Elizabeth jumped and whirled.

No one was there.

Why was she so jumpy?

Elizabeth wound through the shadowy stacks.

The center of the room seemed dark after the bright light splashing in from the windows. Suddenly she saw that she did have company.

A young man with dark hair, an angular face, and a beard sat in a wheelchair, almost hidden by shelves of books. Elizabeth stopped and stared at him for a second. He looked vaguely familiar. As if in response to her gaze, he moved his chair completely behind one of the stacks.

Elizabeth shut the door, crossed the landing to the staircase, and dumped her backpack in front of her. She fished inside it for the aqua silk scarf she had put in there before leaving the dorm that morning.

Elizabeth dug deeper in her pack. No scarf. Well, she must have left it at her desk. She dashed back into the stacks and looked all around the carrel where she had been sitting. Nothing.

"I *know* I put it in the pack this morning," Elizabeth said aloud.

The sound of a soft footstep came again from the twilight surrounding her. Elizabeth swallowed, trying to shake off an irrational feeling of fear.

"I'm being an idiot," she said firmly.

Still, she wanted to get out of there. Elizabeth hurried to the door. She yanked it open so hard that it crashed into the wall, booming into the silence.

"Hey, Elizabeth!" Nina Harper, Elizabeth's best friend at SVU, stood waving at the bottom of the staircase. She was balancing a pile of books in her other arm.

"We're the only two scholars left in the world!" Elizabeth called, forcing her voice to sound cheerful. "I'm coming right down."

I need to get out into the sunshine, she thought. *I've been in here too long.*

The wheelchair rolled slowly behind the dark stacks, then stopped. The dusty air in the library was heating up as noon approached. William White's brown wig was making him sweat. He wiped his arm across his face, accidentally rubbing off some of the brownish makeup he wore to disguise his pale complexion. He looked at his soiled sleeve and frowned.

"Don't forget what you're doing," he said softly to himself. "Don't forget Elizabeth."

The library was perfectly still now that Elizabeth had left. William drew a deep breath and smiled. He'd enjoyed her fear as she'd searched for the scarf.

Slowly he pulled Elizabeth's aqua scarf from his pocket. He let it float across his wrists, then his face. The clean, faint scent of her soap brought back memories of when they had been dating.

"I'll have you again," he whispered. "First in bits and pieces, then all of you. But not until you've waited. Like I have."

He had been so long without her. That was because he'd been in jail, then in a mental institution for trying to kill Elizabeth. Her reporting had exposed him as head of the secret society on campus.

"A society devoted to good works," William said softly. Among other things, the society had kept order, especially between the races—anyone uppity got put in a hospital.

The school authorities thought they'd gotten rid of him for good. William almost laughed. They were stupider than the psychiatrists. He was still at SVU; he was just a part-time employee instead of a student. He couldn't believe how easily fooled the head librarian had been by his fake ID, forged references, and secondhand-store wheelchair. The job she'd offered was beneath him, but it *did* give him the chance to be near Elizabeth.

And he'd managed to work out a nice arrangement at the loony bin. One of the female orderlies at the Harrington Institution opened the door to the locked ward and covered his tracks for him when he had business elsewhere.

Like now. "I finally saw Elizabeth," he said to himself. "She's more beautiful than ever."

He wondered what his feelings were about her now. Anger, yes, because of what she'd done. But he still loved her. She should know that he loved her enough to always find her. He wouldn't try to kill her this time.

Or would he? Kill and love, love and kill. Sometimes they were the same thing.

William seized both ends of the scarf and tied it in a noose. Then he pulled the noose tight.

Chapter Two

Celine Boudreaux accepted a bottle of cold beer from Peter Wilbourne and clinked it loudly against his. "To the new semester," she said, leaning back on the steps of Sigma House.

The sun pleasantly warmed her face. Her thoughts were pleasant, too. For one thing, just being out in the sun instead of cooped up doing her smelly cafeteria job was a relief. And she knew she looked gorgeous in her skintight, mint-green spandex dress. It was important that she look her best. In a few minutes she had an engagement at the library. With someone cold, brilliant, and exciting . . . with William White.

"To the new semester and last night," Peter said, smirking. He took a long swallow of beer.

Celine closed her eyes. What had she done last night? She couldn't remember. Well, she could start with what she did remember. Two days ago she'd gotten a letter from William telling her to stay in touch with Peter. So she'd gone partying with him last night.

The only way to stay in touch with Peter is literally, Celine thought. Peter wasn't much of a conversationalist. And his face was as scratchy as a cactus. But at least she'd had a date.

Anyway, it's just a matter of time before I can diss Peter and cozy up with William in a major way, Celine thought. *In about two minutes I'll be out of here faster than a gator can swim.* There was no comparison between elegant, refined William White and loud, boorish Peter. Except that they were both rich.

Celine smiled to herself. William was so clever. The authorities had thought they'd put him away forever for trying to kill Elizabeth Wakefield.

But where there was a will, there was a way. William always got his way.

A shadow fell across the sun. Celine squinted up. She recognized the shape hanging over her: Paul Richards, her nerd next-door neighbor. They lived in the same apartment building off campus.

"Let's go home," he said abruptly.

Celine took a swig of beer, ran a hand through her thick honey-blond hair, and smiled up at him. "What is that supposed to mean?" she asked, letting Louisiana syrup drip in her voice. Paul was upset. Maybe she could have some fun.

"It means you shouldn't be drinking beer at

ten in the morning," Paul said. "With him," he added, waving a dismissive hand at Peter.

"How about at eleven?" Peter had a very cold look in his pale-blue eyes. "Can she drink with me at eleven?"

"You're coming with me, Celine," Paul said firmly. "Put down the bottle."

Celine stared at him in disbelief. *Put down the bottle?* Who did he think he was to order her around?

"Put down the bottle, Celine," Peter imitated. He snorted. "I want to recycle it."

"How can you drink this early in the morning?" Paul seemed in real anguish. "Especially after last night."

She certainly had gotten around last night, it seemed. Celine tried again to remember where she had been. At a frat party, yes, with loads of noise and people and punch, for a while . . . and then . . . another frat party. Where? Here?

Celine looked up at the towering, Gothic-style frat house behind her. Peter had once been president of Sigma House, but he had been demoted after Elizabeth Wakefield exposed him as a member of the secret society. The school had condemned Celine to live off campus for her involvement in the secret society.

I wasn't even a member of the society, Celine thought for the hundredth time. *I just had the wrong kind of friends—like Peter.*

The school had also assigned her to work in the cafeteria five days a week. That was why the smell of onion rings usually overpowered her Chanel.

Celine gritted her teeth. Sometimes she imagined that everywhere she looked, she saw Elizabeth Wakefield's triumphantly grinning face, floating in trees like the Cheshire cat.

"Go away, Paul," she said. "Go feed your fruit flies." Paul was a dedicated biology major.

"No," he said. "I've already taken care of my subjects for today."

Celine sighed. She wondered if she'd acted like this around William in the past. So in love, so willing to do anything. Well, almost anything.

I did stop short of murder, she reminded herself. *I hope William's got that idea out of his system. I don't like to hang out with raving lunatics.* William's letter, on the gold-crested White family stationery, had seemed rational enough.

"I've had enough of you, punk," Peter said, getting slowly to his feet and hovering over Paul. "Beat it. The *lady* doesn't want you around."

"I'm not leaving without her," Paul said. He folded his arms.

How touching. "Don't get on your white horse for me," she said sourly. What use did she have for Paul? He was short and dorky.

"Where were you last night?" Paul demanded.

"What business is it of yours?"

"I found you staggering around the quad,"

Paul reminded her. "I helped you home. You were singing that stupid song—remember?"

"'He is the darling of my heart, my Southern soldier boy,'" Celine murmured. Now the pieces of the evening were falling into place.

Celine glanced at her watch and stood, brushing off the back of her dress. Those two could dismember each other for all she cared. She was going to William. Still the darling of her heart.

A thin drift of snow blew through the shattered window of the plane onto Lila's face. *I'm so cold,* Lila thought. *It hurts so much.* She fought off waves of blackness and nausea. *Where am I?*

Something was cutting into her ribs. Lila opened her eyes. White sunlight blinded her for a moment. She squinted down. She was still strapped in her seat belt, but she was dangling in midair. For a moment her dazed brain couldn't make sense out of it.

The plane crashed, she thought, running her tongue over her dry lips. So . . . she was hanging there because the plane was upside down—what had been the floor was now the ceiling. Lila stared down at the instrument panel. It was smashed and lifeless.

Her head throbbed and stung. She put her hands to it. To her horror they came away covered with blood. Lila closed her eyes again. She would just sleep until someone came to rescue her.

Cold and pain forced open her eyes again. Her hands and feet were numb from the icy air seeping in through the cracks of the damaged plane.

I have to get out and do something, she thought. *Where's Bruce?* With an aching head she turned to look at the seat dangling broken beside hers.

There was blood there, but he wasn't in it . . . so he was alive somewhere. Unless he had been thrown out on the ground as they had crashed. . . .

Lila swallowed, trying not to throw up. She managed to unfasten the seat belt, and fell to the ceiling of the plane.

"Oh, God!" Lila bit back a scream of agony as broken glass from the shattered instrument panel cut her hands and knees. She sat back on her heels to let the pain die. Bits of glass were embedded in her skin. Frantically she brushed them off. A trickle of blood flowed from one palm.

"This can't be real." Lila gripped her pounding head in her hands and let the tears flow.

They froze and hurt her cheeks. "I can't bear this!" Lila sobbed. "Somebody please help me!"

The ruined plane was silent. Lila shook her head. It hurt when she did that, but the pain cleared it a little. "You have to get out," she ordered herself. "You don't want this to be your grave, do you?"

She had to find out what had happened to Bruce. *No matter how terrible it is,* she thought grimly.

She gripped the handle of the plane door and tried to shove it open. It stuck. Probably the crash had damaged it. So Bruce couldn't have opened it either. That meant he'd been sucked out of the plane through the back or through the broken windows. . . .

Lila sank back down on the plane's ceiling and rested her head on her arms. The image of Bruce's mangled, dismembered body haunted her.

"I can't believe it," she murmured. "That part of this nightmare can't be true."

Blood dripped from her head onto her arm. *It can be true,* she thought wildly, searching for her purse. She needed a bandage. She might be bleeding to death.

Lila stared into the purse. Breath mints; two tubes of lipstick—one coral, one geranium; hair spray. What use was any of that stuff here?

"I have to get out!" she cried.

Lila hurled her shoulder at the door. It flew back. *Superhuman strength,* Lila thought numbly as she climbed out.

Then she gasped. Around the plane was a dead, barren moonscape. Jagged rocks pierced the snowdrifts, jutting at an almost purple sky. The air was so thin, it hurt her lungs to breathe. "People aren't supposed to be here," Lila whispered. Her head pounded so hard she thought she would faint.

She slid to the ground, her back against the

plane. The plane had formed a windbreak, clearing snow from the gray rock ten feet in front of her. Then deep snow began.

Lila's breath caught. A trail of crimson led toward a half circle of rocks about a hundred yards away. Blood . . . Bruce's. What would she find behind those rocks?

"I can't look." Lila shivered and wrapped her arms around herself.

But if Bruce was dying . . . Didn't she owe it to him to comfort him? Wouldn't he do the same for her?

"No, he wouldn't," Lila said between chattering teeth. She walked across the clearing to where the deep snow began. Blood was spattered across the snow, and someone had made deep, indistinct tracks, as if he'd been struggling along.

Lila looked down at her outfit. To get to those rocks and find Bruce, she would have to make it through four-foot drifts in sandals and an evening gown.

"Just do it," she told herself. Her voice quivered in the cold air.

Lila threw herself into the deep snow. The crust of ice on top broke under her weight, dropping her to her waist in drifts. Snow melted into her sandals, and her bare legs ached miserably. The cold instantly penetrated her thin dress to the bone.

Shaking uncontrollably, Lila neared the half

circle of rocks. Broken snow and blood disappeared behind them. *He's back there,* she thought. *Be prepared for a lot more blood.*

She clutched the nearest rock for support as she waded around it. The cold granite stuck to her warm hand and almost tore off the skin. Lila bit her lip hard.

Then she saw him. Lila's screams echoed wildly off the towering, blank white sides of the mountains.

Bruce lay facedown. The snow had turned pink where it melted into his blood. And blood was everywhere: on his arms, legs, and head. Bruce's hands were buried in his darkly stained hair, as though he were trying to hold the life in.

Lila wanted to help him. She wanted to comfort him.

Instead she fainted.

Celine jumped when the wheelchair rolled up behind her. "Is that you, William?" she whispered. It couldn't be . . . except that even with the wrong-color hair, and bad makeup, and tacky clothes, the eyes were the same. As cold and clear as blue ice.

"Don't ever use my name," he said with quiet forcefulness. "Come on. We're going upstairs."

Celine followed him to the elevator. William rolled through the wide door. "So you escaped," she said as soon as the door closed.

"In a manner of speaking." William looked at

the ceiling of the elevator as if he were afraid it was bugged. "But no one knows except you," he added, guiding the chair out at the top floor.

Celine smiled. This was more like it. Maybe, at last, William was realizing how special she was.

William rolled out of the elevator into the top-floor stacks. "I go back to the institution tonight. But first we need to make some plans."

That sounded good. Depending on whether the plans were romantic or just more crazy plots. Celine looked around. Musty, peeling old books and the smell of mold. Cramped study carrels. Not the place she would have picked for their first date.

"Can I smoke in here?" she asked, leaning against a row of metal shelves and flicking her lighter.

"Don't be an idiot!" The cold, controlled mask was off. His face was distorted with anger. "Do you know what will happen to me if I get caught?" William raged. "I'll get thrown in solitary confinement, maybe for years."

Celine stared at him, shocked.

William rubbed a hand over his face. When he took it away, he was wearing a thin smile. "Sorry," he said. "None of this is your fault. I just get so angry at the people at SVU—they stuck me in that institution, and if I get caught here, they'll do it again."

"Why did you come back?" Celine asked, still a little jarred by his outburst. "If anyone finds out you escaped, this is the first place they'll look."

"No one will find out I escaped. I haven't yet, officially." William narrowed his eyes. "I don't like unfinished business. Before I escape for good, I have to take care of Elizabeth."

"How do you mean?" Celine watched him carefully. He'd really gone over the edge about Elizabeth before. Although Elizabeth was probably Celine's least-favorite person in the world—she'd been roommates with Princess Prig most of last semester—Celine didn't want to be part of any more murder plots.

"I just don't like what she did to me." William shrugged. "She got me in a lot of trouble, to put it mildly."

Celine smiled seductively. "I would never get you in trouble, sugar. At least not any trouble you didn't want."

"She got me committed to a mental institution," William went on softly, as though he hadn't heard her. "To an insane asylum. I can't even buy my way out of that place. I've got to reestablish my connections in the outside world."

That sounded like the William she knew. Celine looked him over. She could see beyond present appearances. He would soon enough rise to power again. And if she helped him . . . finally they could be together. She'd be the one in his silver Karmann Ghia, letting the wind whip through her hair as they drove to exclusive restaurants. Their eyes would meet in perfect understanding across the table. Then she'd be dancing slowly in his arms under the soft light of the moon. . . .

"Honey, you don't belong in an insane asylum." Celine was sure of that.

"You're planning to come *this* week?" Billie Winkler said into the phone. She leaned over the living-room couch and rolled her eyes at Steven Wakefield.

"Is that your mother?" Steven asked softly. He stopped washing dishes in the small kitchen of their apartment to listen.

"No, no, it's not an inconvenience if you visit," Billie went on. "I didn't mean that. Of course, we've got classes and stuff." Billie paused. "Did I say 'we'? I meant just me—me and all the other students at SVU."

"Billie, she can't come!" Steven whispered, dropping the dish towel onto the kitchen counter. He walked into the living room and waved his hands to get Billie's attention.

"Um, yeah, that's great," Billie said. She turned her back on Steven. "Just wonderful. Of course it is. Perfect."

She banged down the phone and flopped onto the couch with a groan. "They're coming," she said. "There was nothing I could do."

Steven groaned too. "I can't sleep here, then,"

he said, sitting beside her. "I'll have to hang somewhere else for a few days."

"I guess." Billie raised an eyebrow. "Or I could just tell them once and for all that we're living together."

"I don't think that would be a good idea," Steven said, running a hand through his thick brown hair. "I've met your parents. I think they're already disappointed in me because I don't go to church. I really don't know if they can handle the truth about our relationship."

"But they're coming tomorrow." Billie sighed. "That means they'll be here during classes. I don't want you trying to study while you're camped in the hall."

"I'll go stay with Mike for a couple of days," Steven said. "That's no big deal—he's just one flight down. It's not like I'll be dragging my stuff across town."

Billie frowned. "Steven, we've been lying to my parents for so long about this. It's really starting to bug me. What can they do to me if I tell them you live here? Disown me? Not pay my college tuition?"

"Either of those would be pretty awful," Steven pointed out. "And that really might be what would happen. Let's just plan how to cope with them. Maybe I can sneak down to visit when your parents go to bed."

Billie laughed. "If they caught us, that would

be a great way for them to find out the truth. 'Someone is in bed with my daughter!' shouts my father." She shook her head. "I don't think so, Steven."

"What if I get lonesome?"

"We'll see each other," Billie promised. "Just not between eleven at night and seven in the morning."

"Still, I'll miss you." Steven picked up her hand and kissed it.

Billie gave him a quick kiss. "I'm sorry about this, but there was just no way out of it. They're going to a law conference in L.A., and SVU is a convenient stopover. It's the beginning of the semester, so they know I don't have any exams coming up or papers due yet. We're stuck."

"Oh, it's just for a couple of days," Steven tried to comfort her.

"I don't like kicking you out of your bed." Billie managed a smile. "Thanks for understanding, though."

"I just hope I can get some studying done at Mike's," Steven said. "He's kind of a party guy these days."

"Yeah, I don't see his apartment as being an oasis of quiet," Billie agreed. "The Kawasaki's been roaring in and out of the parking lot at some pretty weird hours. Actually, it's great to see it. Mike couldn't even walk for so long."

Steven looked away. Mike had accidentally shot

himself while he and Steven had been fighting over Jessica. *We're friends now, but I'm not about to forget that I'm half responsible for what happened,* he thought. *And from now on I'm not going to interfere in my little sister's life.*

"There's so much to do," Billie was saying gloomily. "I need to go to the grocery store, and clean, and get your stuff out of sight. . . . Just getting ready for them is going to be exhausting."

"If we're completely careful about what we say and I come over only for dinner, there's no way they'll find out I live here," Steven said firmly. "Everything will be fine."

Chapter Three

"This really is good, you know." Professor Martin pushed back his desk chair and tapped Elizabeth's paper with his finger. "I only gave you a C because I know you can do much better work on the Romantic poets."

Professor Martin leaned forward conspiratorially. His dark eyes twinkled. "So how long did it take you to write that paper, Elizabeth?" he asked. "An hour?"

Elizabeth couldn't help smiling ruefully. "Well, no. Maybe two."

"That's extraordinary. I'd like to see what you can accomplish in three hours." The professor laughed.

"I won't do this again," Elizabeth said quickly. "I've never done such sloppy work before. It was just that my boyfriend and I . . ."

Shut up, she told herself. *Why are you telling*

him all this? Maybe because his expression was so sympathetic, and he was still leaning forward as if to catch her every word.

To cover her confusion, she glanced around Professor Martin's office. His shelves were crammed with poetry books and novels. Books and journals teetered in piles around the door.

Obviously Professor Martin was an expert on literature, even though he seemed to be only a few years older than she was. He looked like a Romantic poet himself, with his longish, wavy dark hair and almost black eyes.

"Let's change this grade to an A." Professor Martin picked up his red pen. "I was only teasing you with the C. Maybe I just wanted an excuse to call you into my office and have someone keep me company on this lovely but dull afternoon. I've been working since early morning."

"Thank you for raising my grade," Elizabeth said, flushing with pleasure. If he'd really wanted an excuse to call her, he must genuinely enjoy her company. He didn't think of her as just an unsophisticated student.

"You know, while I was reading this paper of yours on Shelley, I couldn't help but wonder what you would have to say about my favorite poet."

He swung his chair over to one of the shelves and carefully pulled down a tattered old book. "This is my prize possession."

Lord Byron. Elizabeth ran a finger over the

embossed letters on the faded, cracked leather cover. A chill ran down her spine. She had last read Byron with William White, just a day before he had tried to kill her.

"The work was signed by the poet himself," Professor Martin said proudly. "It's quite valuable."

The dew of the morning/Sunk chill on my brow—/It felt like the warning/Of what I feel now. Elizabeth shook her head to get the last poem she had read with William out of it. "I'm sorry—what did you say?"

"That my great-something grandfather was a friend of Byron's," Professor Martin repeated. "I have my grandfather's diaries, describing their adventures."

"Wow," Elizabeth said admiringly. "He led an amazing life, didn't he?"

Professor Martin put his hands behind his head and nodded. "They fought off the Turks in Greece, sailed in storms, and tried to raise the dead."

Elizabeth sighed. "Modern life seems kind of tame by comparison."

Professor Martin got up and sat on the edge of his desk in front of her. "Well, maybe we could make it a little more interesting. How would you like to work on an individual project with me? I thought of you in connection with my Byron research the minute I finished reading your paper."

"I'd love that," Elizabeth said quickly. Usually only seniors were selected to do special projects with the professors.

"Let's talk after class this week about when we'll work," he suggested. "Maybe late afternoons would be best. Or some evenings. . . . I often have trouble finding any free time during the day."

"I've taken up too much of your time already, Professor Martin," Elizabeth said, jumping to her feet.

"Please, call me George."

"All right . . . George," Elizabeth said shyly.

"I hope you'll enjoy our research together," he added.

"I'm sure I will," Elizabeth said. "I've done a lot of research as a reporter for WSVU. I love it."

"I know. I know all about you," Professor Martin said warmly, walking her to the door. "You're famous on campus, Elizabeth. So let's add to that fame with a paper we can publish in one of the literary journals."

Her first published literary work! "I'd like that," Elizabeth said excitedly. "Thank you so much, Dr. Martin! I mean, George."

"My pleasure," he said. His black eyes held hers for just a second.

Elizabeth hurried down the stairs and outside the English building. The fresh air cooled her face, which was hot with excitement.

I can't wait to get started, she thought. *He has to be the greatest professor at SVU.*

Bryan Nelson had said the Black Students Union meeting would be short. *Good,* Nina Harper thought as she raced across the quad to the social-science building. *I want to get back to my physics homework.* She had left the computer running in the physics lab, waiting for her.

Nina sighed as she yanked open a side door to the building and hurried down the hall. Sometimes she wished her boyfriend weren't the president of the BSU. Maybe then she could have persuaded Bryan to skip the meeting and do something fun, like find a volleyball game at the beach. But instead she would be sitting in a stuffy room at a political meeting.

In the meeting room about a dozen people were sitting around a big table, papers and notebooks scattered in front of them.

"So how have you been, Nina?" asked Rosa Myers, looking up with a smile.

Nina smiled back. "Not bad."

"When are we going to cook Cajun together?" Rosa asked. "I thought we said we would at the meeting last week."

"I don't have much free time until I finish this huge physics project I'm working on," Nina said. She hoped she didn't sound like a nerd. One of her former boyfriends had called her his favorite high-speed computer.

"Whenever you've got the time, I've got the food," Rosa reassured her.

"Soon," Nina promised.

Across the room she noticed Bryan lifting a bound stack of leaflets from the floor. He hadn't seen her yet. His white T-shirt set off his dark skin, and his well-developed arm muscles rippled as he carried the leaflets to the table.

Nina sighed. *He's gorgeous,* she thought.

"Nina!" Bryan's warm hazel eyes, fringed with dark lashes, locked on hers. "You came," he said, sounding relieved.

Nina nodded, still looking into his eyes. They'd had a minor fight at lunch the day before because Nina had tried to get out of the meeting to finish her physics homework. Bryan had accused her of not being committed to the cause.

"I think we're all here now," Bryan said, crossing to the front of the room. "Let's start planning the March Against Racism for next week."

Nina admired him as he talked about the march. She would have admired anyone who had the guts to talk in front of twenty people, and Bryan had the charisma to keep all eyes riveted to him.

"My point is that not enough has been done about the acts of racism committed on this campus," Bryan said, his hazel eyes flashing. "We've raised the issue before the administration and the student government. Now it's time to take it to the people. Let's march!"

The other members nodded or murmured their agreement. The faces of everyone in the room shone with conviction.

These people really want to change the world, Nina thought, feeling guilty. The idea of marching around the campus waving picket signs didn't appeal to her at all. *I guess I just want to understand the world. That's what majoring in physics means.*

"We'll issue an invitation to all the black students on this campus to march with us," Bryan continued. "We'll also ask for support from some of the other colleges and universities in the area. We want the numbers to speak for themselves, as well as our message."

Numbers. A subject Nina knew a lot about. She put up her hand.

"Yes, Nina?" Bryan gave her that heart-melting smile that she would have crossed the Sahara for.

"If we want a lot of people to march against racism, why don't we ask the general student body to join us?" she asked.

Bryan stared at her for a second as if she'd just dropped in from the moon. "I don't think that's a good idea," he said.

"Why not?" Nina asked.

"Nina, they can't," Bryan said, starting to sound exasperated.

"Why not? White people used to be part of

protest marches and sit-ins back in the sixties," Nina said stubbornly.

"That was then and this is now," Bryan said shortly. "We have to show solidarity. Any other business?"

Nina sat again. She'd had a perfectly good idea, and he just shot it down. Rudely, really. As if anything she thought of that contradicted him was just too stupid to be considered. *Does he think I'll march with him after this?* she asked herself angrily.

Nina remembered the computer she'd left running. She picked up her knapsack. "I'm sorry, but I have to leave," she said. She didn't look at Bryan.

He stopped in midsentence.

She headed for the door.

"Nina!" Bryan called. He caught up with her and touched her arm. "Where are you going? You're not mad, are you?"

"A little." Nina knew that twenty pairs of interested eyes were watching them. "Let's discuss it later, OK?"

"I'll come over tonight." Bryan ran his hand down her arm to the tips of her fingers. Then he slowly pulled his hand away.

Nina felt a tingle run up her spine. Her cheeks warmed. *But there's no way I'm going to that march, even if he grovels,* she thought stubbornly as she walked out of the room.

* * *

The phone rang. Steven looked up from his book on Latin American economics and grabbed it off the coffee table. "Hello?"

"Who's this?" asked an older woman's voice.

Billie's mother. *Oh, no,* Steven thought. *Who am I?* Maybe he should assume a false identity. But he couldn't think fast enough. "It's Steven Wakefield, Mrs. Winkler."

"We meet again," Billie's mother joked. "Every time I call, you answer on the first ring."

"Oh, I just stopped by to see Billie before I hit the library," Steven said, trying to sound casual.

"Do you two usually study at the library?" Mrs. Winkler asked.

Steven thought about how he should answer. Every question seemed like a trick one. If he answered wrong, he might give away his and Billie's secret. "We usually hit the library before class in the morning and sometime in the afternoon."

"Hmm," said Mrs. Winkler. "So do you eat breakfast together?"

"No," Steven said firmly.

There was a silence on the other end of the line. Then, "I thought Billie said that you did."

"But not here," Steven said, panicking. "As a matter of fact—" Billie had come out of the bedroom to see who it was. She grabbed the phone.

"Hi, Mom," Billie said. "What? You don't understand our breakfast arrangements? Well, we . . . eat rolls and coffee together in the snack bar." Billie paused. "That's not what I told you the last time you called? What *did* I tell you?"

Steven groaned. Billie wasn't doing any better than he had.

Steven went into the bathroom and shut the door to shut out the words. Maybe he could shut out his stupidity, too. His face was burning with embarrassment. Steven turned on the cold water and splashed some on his face.

"I'm really helping Billie a lot," he told his dripping reflection. "I can just see how this visit is going to go. After two minutes with her parents I'll completely blow her cover. I can't even hold it together over the phone."

Through the door he could faintly hear Billie's voice. She sounded agitated. He'd better get out there and lend moral support.

"So we'll see you soon!" Billie was saying. Her voice was shrill.

"You brave woman," Steven remarked as she hung up.

"I don't see why I have to do this." Billie dropped a limp arm onto the back of the couch. "I guess I salvaged the situation for now. It's just so hard to keep our stories straight. Steven, this isn't going to work."

"Of course it is," Steven said, although he had just been thinking the same thing. "We have to make it work, or your parents will worry about you."

"Why would they worry?" Billie asked. "You're not an ax murderer."

"It's the nature of parents to worry, and yours don't know me very well," Steven said reasonably.

"They will after this visit," Billie said.

"Did Professor Martin show you his old book?" Tom asked Elizabeth jokingly. He almost had to shout to be heard over the screamed greetings and clattering silverware in the snack bar. Most of the campus seemed to be eating dinner there.

"So you know about the Byron too," Elizabeth said, picking up an onion ring from Tom's plate, then setting it down.

"You may have that," Tom said generously, biting into a turkey sandwich.

"Nope," Elizabeth said. "If I gorge on onion rings, I might have bad breath. Then I won't get kissed later."

Tom looked at Elizabeth admiringly. Blond wisps had escaped from her French braid, and her face was flushed a delicate rose color. Tom didn't think she needed to worry about whether she would be kissed.

"I've heard that every student who goes through Martin's hands has to sit through the Byron-book lecture," he said. "It's a rite of passage."

"Well, he and I had an in-depth conversation

about it, since I have a special interest in Romantic poetry." Elizabeth stirred a teaspoon of sugar into her black coffee. "Professor Martin has asked me to do an independent study with him."

"Wow." Tom raised an eyebrow. "That's being singled out, isn't it?"

Elizabeth beamed. "I guess so," she said. "He liked that paper I wrote on Shelley. You remember—the one I almost forgot to write at all? I thought it was a disaster, but Dr. Martin thought it was great—he changed my grade to an A."

"From the way your face is lit up, I'd guess you told him you want to do the project?" Tom looked thoughtfully at the dreamy expression on Elizabeth's face.

"Tom," Elizabeth laughed, "of course I'm doing the project. Who would be crazy enough to pass up such an incredible opportunity to work with George—er, Professor Martin?"

"Yeah," Tom answered. "Who?"

Elizabeth bent to sniff a tea rose in the campus rose garden.

"'I arise from dreams of thee in the first sleep of night,'" she quoted. "'The winds are breathing low and the stars are burning bright. . . .'" Shelley. One of the greatest Romantic poets.

Elizabeth turned down a row of spectacular orange-and-yellow roses. She could almost taste their heavy scent. The English were famous for their gardens. She imagined herself in England, visiting the great manor houses where the poets had lived. Strolling through sculpted gardens, arm in arm with . . . Professor Martin.

Professor Martin? What was she thinking? Why not Tom?

Because Tom wouldn't want to go to England and wander through poets' gardens. "Of course he would," she said to herself. "If he knew it was important to me, he'd want to. Even if he isn't all that interested in Romantic poets."

It would be great to see English gardens with Tom, she assured herself quickly. Tom was wonderful company. She could imagine the two of them staying in a cozy bed-and-breakfast together, eating fresh-baked bread and taking long bike rides. Anyway, it wasn't as if Professor Martin would go with her to England. That wasn't even a possibility.

Elizabeth looked up and saw Nina working her way down a row of tiny white bud roses. "Hey, Nina!" she called.

"Hey, Liz." Nina let go of the flower she was smelling and joined Elizabeth in front of the pink King's Ransoms.

"You look upset," Elizabeth said. "What's wrong?"

"Bryan and I had another argument about politics." Nina shook her head. "This one was right out in public today at the BSU meeting. He embarrassed me in front of twenty people."

Elizabeth made a face. "That doesn't help a relationship."

"That's the understatement of the semester," Nina said.

"What are you going to do?" Elizabeth bent to smell a deep-red Medallion rose.

"I haven't decided." Nina scowled. "I'm trying just to cool off before I decide anything."

"Very wise," Elizabeth said, nodding.

"Yeah, but I don't feel like being wise." Nina shrugged. "After what he did, he doesn't deserve to talk to me when I'm all cool and collected. He deserves to get shouted at."

"So are you going to see him later?" Elizabeth asked. Nina looked unhappy and flustered. *Usually she's so perfectly in control,* Elizabeth thought. *Bryan must really have hurt her feelings.*

Nina shook her head. "I have to study now that I've wasted this much time cooling off. Enough about my love life. What are you mooning about while you stop and smell the roses?"

"For once, not Tom. I'm thinking about a new project. My English professor asked me to work with him on studying the Romantic poets."

"Wow, that's right up your alley."

"It might be just what I need. I'll spend less time just hanging out, and more time thinking about poetry, like Professor Martin. He has a poetic soul," Elizabeth said, gazing at the sky. The sun was setting in magnificent banners of gold behind the gardens.

"Bryan has a political soul," Nina said wryly. "I have a scientific soul. Maybe our relationship is hopeless."

"I thought Tom had a poetic soul. He wrote me a beautiful poem once." Elizabeth frowned. "But he hasn't written me any more."

"For a while there last semester you were getting too much written stuff." Nina raised an eyebrow. "Are you still getting those screwy notes from that guy who said he's coming for you?"

"No." Elizabeth stooped to run her hand over the emerald-green grass they were walking on. "The last note said 'not long now,' and I got a couple of creepy calls at home over Christmas. I was looking over my shoulder all the time, but nothing happened."

"That's a relief. Sounds like he's disappeared."

"Yeah. I hope he's crawled back under a rock."

Chapter Four

Lila regained consciousness and slowly pushed herself to a sitting position. "Oh, my God!" she screamed. Bruce was still lying dead in front of her.

She struggled to her feet. "I have to get away from him!" she said hoarsely. Anywhere, just *away* . . .

Her legs were numb. Lila's ankles caved in as she tried to run. She forced herself to plow on through the snow. The sharp edges of the ice on top were actually cutting her legs, she realized dimly.

"I need to rest," she whispered. She stopped and looked around.

The sun was dipping behind the barren western peaks, turning the ice a glistening violet. A bitter wind was picking up. Soon it would be dark. She'd be all alone, in the terrible cold. With Bruce dead out there.

The dwarf trees shivered. Something was thrashing toward her through them. *God, there must be bears out here, and mountain lions and wolves. . . .*

Lila turned to run. Her dress caught on a rock and tore. Whatever was behind her was coming up fast, its paws crunching on the refreezing snow.

The snow broke under each of her steps. She could hardly move. *I don't want to die,* Lila thought frantically.

"Lila! Wait!"

Bruce's voice. She was going insane. He was dead. But her ribs hurt too much to run anymore. She slowly turned.

"I can't believe it! You're alive!" Bruce was struggling through the drifts.

Lila stared at him, unable to make sense out of anything. Then she knew. Her body shook, and she could hardly breathe the frigid, thin air. They'd both died, and this was the afterlife.

The cold was devouring her face, lungs, and legs. They stung and throbbed. So the afterlife was a cold hell.

Bruce caught up to her in the snow. Lila gazed at his familiar face. Tears filled her eyes. No, it really was he. Big, alive, and reassuring. Bruce grabbed her and hugged her hard. Lila hugged him back. She'd never been so glad to see anyone. *I'm not alone. Bruce isn't dead.*

She choked on a sob. "What were you doing out there?" she managed to ask.

"Trying to figure out where we are. I must have passed out." Bruce's face was pale. His forehead was cut, and a slow trickle of blood dropped to the snow from his fingers. "Let's get back to the plane and try to warm up," he said. "We'll freeze out here. Especially you. God, Lila, you've got on sandals. Are you crazy or something?"

Lila was afraid to look at her feet. They must be purple and frostbitten. "You . . . looked so terrible when I found you," she stammered. "You were all bloody."

"You don't look so hot yourself." Bruce waded back through their tracks toward the plane.

Don't cry, Lila said to herself. *The last thing you want to do is have a major breakdown in front of Bruce Patman.*

"How badly hurt are you?" he asked over his shoulder.

"I don't know. I guess it's not too bad or I couldn't walk."

"Me either."

"Do you know where we are?" she asked. Maybe he did, and someone would come rescue them tonight.

"Somewhere in the Sierra Nevada." Bruce looked around. "Somewhere very lost. I don't know."

Lila sniffled. Her hair was wet and half-frozen

from lying in the snow. *I'll catch cold,* she thought. Then she bit her tongue to keep from laughing hysterically. *Like it matters. I'll probably freeze to death tonight, and I'm worried about catching a cold. . . .*

"We've got to change out of these wet clothes," Bruce said when they got to the plane. "Go ahead. I don't think there's room for both of us to turn around in there."

"Thanks." It was weird that they could have changed together if there had been room, Lila thought numbly. Who cared? Out here was a new universe. Little things like seeing Bruce naked didn't matter when you probably had only a few hours to live.

Lila climbed through the wreckage in the cockpit and back into the plane's small passenger section. She rummaged through her overnight bag. She needed two things: warm, dry clothes and something to use to bandage Bruce's hand. Good, her mind was working again.

She sat back. She'd brought only jeans and T-shirts to spend the weekend at her parents'. Those wouldn't be much good in the subzero temperatures tonight. Lila swallowed.

Maybe Bruce had something she could borrow. Lila opened his suitcase and rooted through his clothes. She pulled out flowered tropical-weight shirts and shorts. "Where was he going?" she muttered. "Obviously he wasn't planning on snowshoeing this weekend either."

Ah! Sweatpants and sweatshirts. Thank God. Lila slipped on a sweatshirt, forcing her shaking, numb hands through the sleeves. She could smell Bruce's scent on it: aftershave mixed with sweat. Strange, but reassuring. Something from home that didn't remind her of blood and cold and death.

Lila peeled off her shredded stockings and closed her eyes. *Just look,* she insisted. *They can't be worse than you're imagining.*

Her feet were red and chapped and hurt, but they were still there. Not black and falling off from frostbite. Lila uttered a silent prayer of thanks.

Lila yanked on a pair of Bruce's big socks. What else could she use to get warm?

"My hiking boots! I brought my hiking boots!" She had planned to take some hikes in the hills around campus. Tears of joy filled Lila's eyes.

She had matches in her purse. Lila crawled back to the cockpit and pulled her purse from beneath a pile of shattered glass. She shook it off and climbed out of the plane.

Bruce brushed by her and pulled himself through the hatch.

She'd forgotten his bandage. "Hand me my dress, would you?" Lila called. She leaned into the plane. Bruce was pulling off his wet, bloodstained black T-shirt, revealing his muscular shoulders. He grabbed a navy sweatshirt from the back of one of the passenger seats, quickly put it on, and tossed her the dress.

Lila caught it and stared at it for a second. This had been a fabulous designer dress. She'd shopped for hours before she'd finally found it in a boutique near Hollywood Boulevard. Now it was torn and ruined.

Lila ripped it in two. Why not make it into a bandage? That was what was important now. She might never go to a party again.

Don't think like that, she told herself, shaking her head.

Night was falling fast. Lila could barely make out the ragged edges of the mountains against the midnight-blue sky.

Bruce jumped out of the plane and slapped his hands together. "We need a fire," he said.

Lila held up the matches.

Bruce nodded. "Great. I'll get some brush."

Lila arranged the branches and twigs he brought and quickly lit a fire. "Let's bandage your hand," she said as he dumped another load of wood next to her.

"The bleeding's almost stopped. I just hope it doesn't open up again." Bruce held out his arm.

Lila wrapped the bandage around his wrist. She hoped she remembered from her Red Cross class how to do it without cutting off the circulation.

Bruce watched her work. "I guess we're going to live," he said.

"I don't know." The icy wind stung Lila's cheeks. She tied a neat knot in the bandage and reached to put more branches on the fire.

"This feels great." Bruce warmed his hands over the fire.

No, this feels bizarre, Lila thought, watching the orange firelight play over Bruce's handsome face. She remembered her nightmare of crashing in a plane and being consumed in a fireball. But she hadn't died in the actual crash, so the dream hadn't completely foretold the future. What would happen now?

The night was very black. The stars hung, clear and bright in the thin air. A faint howl echoed between the mountaintops. Lila shivered.

"When do you think somebody will come looking for us?" she asked. "My parents think I'm at school, and I told Jess I was planning to go to a spa with my mother." Lila chewed her bottom lip, struggling to suppress the wave of panic that was threatening to overwhelm her.

"Well, no one's going to miss me for weeks. I told my frat brothers and my parents I was going to Acapulco." Bruce laughed harshly and kicked the snow. "This isn't exactly Mexico, is it?"

"So no one will come looking for us?" Terror was rising in Lila's throat again, about to bubble into hysterical screams.

The firelight gleamed off Bruce's fine features. He picked up a stick and poked the flames. "No," he said. "They won't."

"Do you want to dance?" Jessica screamed at James Montgomery over the thumping, rocking noise of the sound system at Sigma House. This was her idea of a party: wild music, an excited crowd of pumped-up people dancing, and the most desirable man on campus at her side.

James laughed. "If we can find a space on the dance floor!" he shouted over the crash of drums.

"What?" Jessica screamed back.

James shook his head and grinned at her. He grabbed her hand and pulled her into the dancing crowd.

A kaleidoscope of spotlights turned the dancers orange, blue, and green. James held Jessica close, pressing her against him as they danced a wide, leisurely circle.

"Did I tell you I'm going to be a Theta again?" Jessica asked, putting her mouth close to his ear. "All I have to do is some stupid challenge to prove my loyalty."

"I knew they'd ask you to repledge." James smiled back. "Let's just say that some of the Sigma brothers weren't too happy when we heard there was any doubt you would be asked. We mentioned that to the Theta officers."

There was certainly no doubt in Jessica's mind

that she would be a Theta now, whatever Alison had planned for her. The Sigmas' wishes were too important to be ignored. Jessica smiled and looked deep into James's sky-blue eyes. She also had no doubt that she and James were going to mean something very special to each other.

The beat of the music quickened. James flung Jessica into the rhythm. The heavy thud of the bass guitar and the precise way their bodies moved together made Jessica's heart race.

The music stopped.

"I'm going to get some soda and say hi to Isabella," Jessica said, touching James's shoulder. "Be right back."

"Don't be long." James squeezed her hand. "I'll be hanging over there with my frat brothers." James gestured at a group of Sigmas. One of them was sliding down the banister from the second floor with no hands while the crowd below cheered.

At the refreshment table Isabella and Danny Wyatt, her boyfriend, were sharing a big bag of sour-cream potato chips. Isabella's pale complexion contrasted with Danny's dark skin. Jessica thought they were a great-looking couple.

"Dance, Danny," Jessica said, getting a club soda out of the cooler and twisting open the cap. "I haven't seen you out there all night. Don't be a nerd."

"Hey, I'm just conserving energy right now.

I'll be executing some fancy moves before this party's over."

"James is a hot dancer, Jess," Isabella chimed in. "You guys looked pretty friendly out there. So pardon my nosiness, but are you two an official item now?"

Jessica took a drink of her soda. "Not yet," she said. "I like James a lot. He's a great athlete, and he's very sensitive and understanding. To say nothing of his looks."

"Do I sense a 'but' coming?" Danny interrupted.

"*But* I'm going to be really careful before I get involved with anyone again."

"I can understand that," Isabella said, nodding.

No, you can't, Jessica thought. *You've never been married. Your husband never threatened to beat you up. Your brother and husband didn't almost kill each other.* Only Lila, recently a widow, could come close to understanding the anguish Jessica still sometimes felt over the annulment of her marriage to Mike.

Alexandra Rollins reached around Isabella and dipped a big plastic cup into the punch bowl.

Jessica arched an eyebrow. "That stuff is spiked, Alex."

"That's the idea," Alex muttered. She walked unsteadily off.

"She's already had a few." Isabella shook her head.

"A few too many," Danny said disapprovingly.

What's with Alex tonight? Jessica wondered. *I thought she'd managed to snag dull Todd away from Elizabeth.*

Scanning the room, Jessica caught sight of Todd Wilkins, Elizabeth's old boyfriend. He was watching Elizabeth with a wistful expression. Elizabeth didn't notice. She was perched on the back of the couch with some of the other WSVU staff, laughing at something Tom had said.

Oh, Jessica thought, nodding. *There's Alex's problem. Todd is still gaga over Liz.* Jessica knew that Alexandra didn't stand a chance with Todd until he believed that he truly had no hope of winning Elizabeth back. *Poor Alex. I'm the first to admit that it's not easy to compete with one of the Wakefield twins!*

The music started up again with a blast.

"Imagine, Liz is at a fraternity party!" Jessica yelled to Isabella. "How can she stand it? Everyone's having a good time—no one is talking about poetry, or the environment, or their serious concerns about the governor's race. . . ."

"Hey, where's Lila?" Isabella yelled. "She's missing the party of the year!"

"I think she and her mother went to a spa!" It was strange to be forming words that Jessica couldn't hear over the throb of the guitars.

Isabella tugged on Danny's hand. "Come on, Danny. Let's dance!"

Danny took her hand, and they disappeared into the crowd.

"Are you alone?" James said in a sexy voice from behind Jessica.

"Not anymore," Jessica answered, turning with a smile.

James bent to kiss her cheek and run his hand casually through her silky golden hair.

I hope a lot of people are looking, Jessica thought.

Out of the corner of her eye, she could see that they were.

A group of Theta sisters were sitting on the stairs to the second floor.

Excellent. Jessica smiled at them. Then her smile froze.

Alison Quinn was gripping the banister, staring at her. There was pure, undisguised hatred in her gaze.

Jessica felt a shiver go down her spine.

Nina saw Bryan standing on the other side of the dance floor at the frat house. He hadn't seen her yet.

Good. "I should leave," Nina said to herself. "Then we won't have an unpleasant scene."

But why should she worry about that? *She* wasn't going to be unpleasant. If he came over, she'd just walk away.

Bryan spotted her and waved.

After a second Nina waved back.

Bryan headed toward her with his usual athletic, purposeful walk.

Nina looked for the nearest exit. By the time she saw it behind all the dancing bodies, Bryan was beside her.

"Hi!" he yelled.

Nina just nodded. She'd been at the party only a few minutes, and already her throat hurt from screaming hello to people.

"Great party!" Bryan shouted.

Nina nodded again. *Has he completely forgotten about the way I walked out of the meeting today?* she thought. *He certainly didn't come rushing over to the dorm to apologize.*

"Excuse me!" she screamed, trying to push by him toward the door.

Bryan gripped her arm and drew her close. *"What?"*

He was just pretending he couldn't hear her. Wasn't he? "I have to go study!" Nina shouted, using up her last bit of voice.

"I'd love to dance," Bryan said, pulling her toward the dance floor. "Glad you asked."

Nina groaned silently. Sure, he misunderstood. He was getting his way with her again.

Just as they faced each other to dance, the music changed to a slow number.

Bryan held out his hands.

Nina hesitated, then put her arms around him.

The music washed over her like a soothing warm tide. Bryan's hands went down her back, pressing her close to him. Nina lost herself in the movement of their bodies, the heavy, intimate air of the party, and the crisp, masculine scent of aftershave on Bryan's face, so near her own.

The song ended. "Is everything OK now?" Bryan asked.

"No," Nina said. She couldn't believe he thought he could get back on her good side with just one dance, instead of admitting he'd been wrong to insult her at the meeting. Been wrong not to *agree* with her at the meeting.

The thing was, she was almost ready to fall into his arms again anyway. Nina broke away from him and ran out onto the porch. The cool night air washed over her hot face like a refreshing dip in a swimming pool.

Elizabeth and Tom came out on the porch the same time as Bryan. They almost collided in the doorway as Bryan rushed through. "Hi, Nina," Elizabeth said, looking quizzically at Bryan. "Do you guys want to come with us for a pizza? This party is too crowded to be much fun."

"Sounds good to me," Bryan said, moving closer to Nina.

"I can't come," Nina said, more abruptly than she'd meant to.

Elizabeth looked from one to the other. "Sure?"

Nina sighed. She hadn't told Elizabeth that she and Bryan were still fighting. Nina had thought Bryan would have apologized by now. And of course, given the way they'd just been dancing, no one would exactly have suspected they were bitter enemies.

"Of course we want to go," Bryan said, in the same bossy tone he'd used to shoot down her idea at the BSU meeting that morning.

"I'm sure I *don't* want to go," Nina said.

"I'm really hot," James said in Jessica's ear. "Let's go outside for a little while."

"OK." Jessica took his hand. "I wouldn't mind breathing again." The acrid smell of cigarette smoke clung to her clothes and throat.

They stood outside on the porch, inhaling the salty fresh air. James ran his hand lightly up and down Jessica's back.

Jessica shivered and wrapped her arms around him. James kissed her lightly. Then his mouth became warm and searching on hers.

Jessica's whole body answered his kiss, moving in his strong arms. She lost herself in the touch of his delicious soft lips and the astonishingly gentle tickle of his fingers on her back.

Suddenly Jessica stiffened. James's kiss had turned hard and demanding. His hands began wandering places she didn't want them to.

Jessica tried to push him away gently. He

didn't stop. The kiss began to hurt, and he was pulling the back of her silk shirt out of her jeans.

No, she thought. *Why is he doing this?*

His hands reached under the shirt.

Jessica shoved him as hard as she could. He staggered back, catching himself on the porch railing.

James stared at her, breathing fast. For a second Jessica thought he'd forgotten who she was. "I'm going in," he said, and turned and went through the door before she could answer.

Jessica rubbed her lips.

Maybe she should leave. But that would be overreacting. Wouldn't it?

He just got carried away, she thought. *He'll apologize.* Jessica took a deep breath and opened the door to the frat house.

Inside, the stale air choked her. Jessica saw James across the room, laughing and clowning with some of the Sigmas.

She frowned. Obviously James didn't think what had happened was any big deal. Maybe she shouldn't either.

So he was a little rough, Jessica thought. *I guess guys are sometimes. Other than that, James is absolutely perfect.*

Chapter Five

The sun was shining on a spectacular morning. A bird sang sweetly in a nearby tree.

And I'm making an idiot out of myself again, Winston Egbert thought, flailing his arms as he tried to keep his balance. *What kind of sadistic mind invented Rollerblades?*

"Come on, Winnie!" Denise Waters skated backward and held out her hands. Winston tried to grab them and almost fell forward onto the sidewalk.

Denise did a jump. Winston clumsily skated after her, working up some speed. The green lawns at the front of the campus snaked by him. He wondered how to stop. Never mind; he probably wasn't going fast enough to have to worry about it.

"Winston!" A group of girls from his hall waved at him. Winston looked over his shoulder and waved back.

The lapse in concentration was a mistake. Winston fell over backward, painfully bouncing on his tailbone. Denise skated up to him. Her beautiful blue eyes were twinkling.

"I forgot to tell you—sitting on the ground isn't part of Rollerblading," she said.

"Very funny," Winston grumbled. "Aren't you going to help me up? Some girlfriend you are."

Denise took both his hands and hauled him up. Winston almost pulled the two of them over in the process.

"Hi, Winston!" A girl from his English class was standing just behind his elbow, smiling at him.

"Stay back," Winston warned. "You're in the hazard zone. I could fall anywhere within about ten feet square."

"Oh, Winnie, you're so silly." The girl laughed and walked away.

"You're just too *much,* Winnie." Denise imitated the girl's voice.

Winston looked cautiously at Denise. She seemed a little mad. He didn't know why. Surely she couldn't be jealous. Denise was the most beautiful, intelligent, sophisticated woman on campus. And he was Winston Egbert, class clown.

"Is something wrong?" he asked.

"Nope." Denise kissed his nose. "You're just spoiled. Since you live in an all-female dorm, you get twenty-four-hour-a-day female attention at home. And I think it's catching: Every woman on campus knows who you are."

"Really?" Winston said hopefully.

Denise smacked his arm and took off on her blades. "Race you!" she shouted over her shoulder.

Winston stared after her. He'd had a really great time with Denise last night, watching old Charlie Chaplin videos and eating barbecue potato chips and other junk food.

Now it was payback time, Winston realized. The laws of physics were kicking in: For every action there must be an equal and opposite reaction. Have the time of your life, break your neck on skates. Made perfect sense.

Winston put down his head and awkwardly shoved himself across the concrete. This was, he knew, supposed to be fun.

Todd Wilkins stood ahead of him, waving two notebooks like racing flags. Suddenly Winston felt a little inspired. He couldn't catch Denise, but he could give her a run for her money. He pumped the blades harder.

The palm trees next to the sidewalk shot by him in a blur.

Then, suddenly, they were coming right at him. Winston threw up an arm in self-defense.

An enormous palm tree smashed into him. Winston felt something splinter. Himself or the tree? Pain roared through him like a freight train.

"Winston!" Denise screamed. "Oh, God!"

* * *

Lila woke to a brilliant orange sunrise. Where was she? The light wasn't this intense in Sweet Valley.

The plane had crashed . . . her head still hurt a little . . . but she was warm.

She was in Bruce Patman's arms. Lila jerked back and stumbled to her feet. Bruce rolled over and groaned. Maybe he hadn't realized they'd accidentally slept together like that.

Lila stared down at him. Bruce had a two-day shadow of dark beard, and his hair was rumpled. He looked like a trapper or some other kind of adventurer. The effect wasn't bad.

"What the hell's going on?" he said, propping himself up on his elbows.

"We're lost." Lila stared at the mountains, lit by the rising sun like cold orange volcanoes. Countless peaks of ice stretched before her. How many of those peaks did they have to cross to get home?

"This situation is hopeless," Bruce said, yawning and rubbing his stubbled chin.

"No, it isn't," Lila said angrily, because she'd been thinking the same thing. "We'll just have to walk down. People have done it in the movies."

"Oh, really, Lila—in the movies. I'm glad to hear that," Bruce said sarcastically. "Did it occur to you there might be a difference between watching some actors prance around a movie set in

Hollywood on an inch of made-to-order snow, and trying to hike out of the Sierras in the dead of winter?" Bruce straightened his blood-encrusted bandage.

"What other choice do we have?" Lila demanded. "Although—wait. The traffic-control center at Sweet Valley will find us. They'll check your flight plan and find out you never landed where you were supposed to."

"I didn't file one." Bruce looked away.

"What!" Lila shouted. "That's idiotic. Any pilot knows to always, *always* file a flight plan!"

He was going to kill her with his stupidity. *I've always hated him,* she thought.

"I hadn't decided exactly where I was going, OK?" Bruce said angrily.

"No, it isn't OK!"

"Wait a minute." Bruce jumped to his feet. "Did you try the radio?"

"No," Lila said excitedly. "Do you think it still works?"

"I hope so," Bruce muttered, running over to the plane. "We could be out of here by lunchtime if it does."

Lila crossed her fingers in the pockets of her sweatshirt. "Please work, please work," she prayed. She tried not to think about the shattered, smashed instrument panel, where the radio was.

"It's dead!" Bruce shouted.

Lila slumped against the plane. *So are we,* she thought. Tears filled her eyes.

"Let's eat." Bruce stepped out of the cockpit. "I've got your bag of food."

They sat down next to the ashes of their campfire.

Lila bit into a sandwich. The normal, tasty food, prepared by her mother, made her feel better.

She wiped away her tears. All right. No one would come looking for them. That was the situation Bruce had stuck her with.

Lila looked down the mountainside. It was bare for about half a mile, and covered with deep, drifted snow. Then a forest of dark-green pine trees began. It stretched away into the distance as far as she could see. Trees growing meant it was warmer down there. And beyond those trees was home.

"I really don't know what we should do now," Bruce said somberly.

Lila finished her sandwich. Bruce had a knapsack with him; they could put the food in there, and extra clothes, and the skinny flight blankets and pillows.

Lila took a deep breath. The cold air burned her lungs. "Come on," she said. "Let's start walking."

Seven A.M., Jessica thought. She yawned, combing her silky hair with her fingers. *I am not a morning person.* Maybe this was the real challenge she had to meet for the Thetas—to be at the sorority house at the crack of dawn with a happy face. She'd partied till four in the morning, and now Jessica's eyes felt like tiny, puffy slits.

At Theta House Alison ordered Jessica to sit in the same chair in the dining room that she'd sat in the day before. It was starting to feel like the electric chair. When Alison left the room, Jessica wondered if she'd gone to pull the switch.

Alison's playing mind games, she thought. *But I guess this is all part of rushing a sorority.*

Alison hurried in with Tina, one of the freshman pledges. They wore colorful, expensive-looking sundresses. Tina was laughing at something Alison had said.

"Are you ready to hear your challenge, Jessica?" Tina asked, smoothing back her highlighted blond hair.

"Yes," Jessica said, trying to act calm. *Yes, I am, Little Ms. Suck Up. Who do you think* you *are to give me the challenge?* Those pretty sundresses were definitely wasted on their owners, Jessica decided. Alison was a dried-out stick, and Tina had mousy brown hair and a long, plain face.

The other sisters were trickling into the dining room to hear the announcement of what Jessica was going to have to do. Isabella was frowning. *Not a good sign,* Jessica realized.

Alison pulled up a chair in front of Jessica's.

"We need you to steal just one little book. Simple, really. That isn't very much to prove your loyalty to the Thetas, is it?"

Jessica took a deep breath. "No," she said.

Alison was watching her closely. *She's trying not to laugh,* Jessica realized. *She thinks I'll chicken out. Well, I won't.*

Alison flipped up an immaculately manicured hand. "Don't worry; you're not stealing the book for good. You'll put it back later. Of course, we want to help you all we can in performing this challenge." Alison took a screwdriver out of her dress pocket. "You'll need this to break into the office."

"W-what office?" Jessica stammered. She had expected the test to be something embarrassing but harmless, like singing rock songs from the roof of the sorority house. *What will happen to me if I get caught?* Jessica wondered.

"Professor Martin's office," said Alison coolly. "The challenge is to steal his signed edition of Byron and bring it back to the sorority house. By tomorrow."

The other sisters gasped.

"That's too soon!" Jessica protested. She felt the room spin a little. How could she possibly do this?

"Tomorrow," Alison said dismissively. "Or forget about being a Theta, Jessica. This is your last chance."

* * *

There's a lot of stuff going on at this school, Tom thought, staring at the blue computer screen in his office at WSVU. *And little by little, I intend to expose all of it with SVU's star reporter, Elizabeth Wakefield.*

Tom heard someone come up behind him. "Figuring out how to leap tall buildings in a single bound Mr. Watts?"

Tom turned with a smile. "With a little help from my beautiful girlfriend, the sky's the limit."

Elizabeth sat down and propped her chin on her hands. "So tell me your brilliant ideas."

"Hmm. Let's see." Tom swiveled in his chair to face her. "We need some inspiration. You know, you could come over here and kiss me."

Elizabeth stood, walked over, and brushed his lips with her own.

"Did I tell you I'm working on another poem for you?" Tom asked. "It's hard going, though. . . . I'd much rather just come find you and show you how I'm feeling these days."

Elizabeth's mouth found his in a heart-stopping kiss. Her body molded itself to his. Tom closed his eyes, running his thumbs over the soft skin of her cheeks, smoothing his hands down her neck, then under her shirt to touch her velvet, fine-boned shoulders.

Elizabeth broke away. They were both breathing as if they'd run a marathon.

"You've really got self-control," Tom said grudgingly.

"We were about to go too far." Elizabeth straightened her shirt and tucked in the back.

Tom nodded noncommittally. That was the point—he wanted to go further. *But I'd never want her to do something that made her feel uncomfortable,* he thought. *Guys like that make me sick.*

"It's miles to civilization, through blizzards and forests full of wild animals," Bruce complained. "Man, I'm exhausted."

Lila was too tired to speak. They'd been walking since early morning. They'd reached the trees farther downhill from the plane, but the snow was still deep. It kept breaking under her weight, dropping her into holes almost to her waist.

The sun glared off the snow in a million tiny, twinkling diamonds. Lila concentrated on putting one foot before the other. She tried not to think how many more times she would have to do it before she got back to a warm, soft bed.

"The way's easier over here," Bruce called.

Lila turned. A smooth path cut through the rocks and trees, leading straight down as far as she could see. The slope looked like a perfectly groomed ski run.

Bruce was already walking down it. He wasn't falling through, either—the snow was packed.

Lila began walking behind Bruce near the edge

of the wide white path. The lack of trees was almost eerie.

"This isn't so bad," Bruce said.

It really wasn't. Lila got into the rhythm of walking. The sun-warmed air smelled of pine and clean melting snow. A bird chirped at the top of a tree.

The ground trembled.

She was imagining things. How could that be? She kept going.

Then Lila heard a strange rumbling, growling sound. The ground shook harder.

"Thunder?" Bruce said wonderingly. He looked behind them. Lila saw his eyes widen in terror.

She swung around quickly. A churning, roaring sea of snow was hurling down the mountain. A heavy mist of snow blotted out the blue sky. Huge trees to the sides of the trail were falling like matchsticks.

"Run!" Lila screamed. "*Run!* It's an avalanche!"

"They're coming!" Billie shrieked from the doorway of the bedroom. "Steven, you've got to leave right away. My parents will be here any minute!"

Steven dropped the book he was reading and sat up on the bed. He struggled to untangle himself from the covers. "What? *Now?* I thought—"

"Get off the bed! And hide this stuff—put it

away or something!" Billie ran around the bedroom, grabbing fistfuls of dirty socks and underwear. "My parents know I don't wear Jockey shorts!"

"They're supposed to be coming late tonight," Steven muttered, flinging open a drawer. It was already jammed to the top with shirts. He shoved it shut. "Can't you tell them to wait?"

"They're at the airport, which is fifteen minutes away. I couldn't tell them to just keep driving around for a couple of hours while I hide my boyfriend and his laundry. Steven, what am I going to do? There is definitely a man living here." Billie pointed at Steven's dirty clothes littering the floor and the collection of bats and balls in the corner.

Steven walked over, took her shoulders, and turned her around. "I'll deal with the bedroom," he said. "Pick up the rest of the house."

"How?" Billie wailed. "I think your hair is all over the place!"

Her panic was contagious. "I don't know!" Steven said, hurrying to the closet and pulling out a couple of suitcases. He ran over and thrust a suitcase into her hand. "Here. Throw anything you find in here. Or the closets."

Billie raced off with the suitcase. Steven opened the other one on the bed. What would he need at Mike's? He tossed in shirts and jeans, not wasting time folding them. Books.

The suitcase filled up too fast. What had Billie just done with his underwear? Steven looked under the bed. Nothing but an outrageous amount of dust and two Ping-Pong balls. How did they get there?

Steven backed out from under the bed and ran to the living room to ask Billie where she had put his underwear. Looking like a wild woman, she was hurling magazines addressed to him into the open suitcase.

"Put on some clothes!" Steven shouted. "Didn't you notice you're half dressed?"

The doorbell rang. Billie kicked the suitcase shut and rushed at Steven. She pushed him into the bedroom and then into the closet.

Steven opened his mouth to protest. Billie slammed the closet door. Then it opened again and she shoved in his suitcase. A pair of Steven's Jockeys whisked under the door.

Silence.

"Mom, Dad, it's so good to see you," Billie said.

Chapter Six

The snow was suffocating Lila like a blanket. *I'm buried alive!* she screamed, but no sound came out. Thick, choking snow filled her mouth. Her lungs ached for air. She clawed madly at the white prison.

She was blacking out. *Fight!* she thought desperately, but her body no longer obeyed.

Was that a glimmer of brightness just beyond her left hand? The snow was melting in her eyes. With her last strength she forced her hand through the heavy layer. Light poured into the hole.

A strong hand gripped hers, hauling her through the snowy grave. In seconds she was standing shakily, gasping in pure air.

"Lila!" Bruce's hands were on her shoulders. Lila collapsed into his arms.

"I can't believe you're alive." Bruce's voice

shook. "God—I saw you *buried*. I thought I'd never find you. Everything's covered with snow now."

Lila turned her head. The slope was no longer smooth. Boulders of snow lay everywhere in jagged heaps. "They probably wouldn't even have been able to find my body," she said, shuddering.

Lila looked up into Bruce's face. He had a funny expression. Sort of concerned, maybe bewildered. He was so close. . . . His blue eyes looked into hers. The snow had settled and the blue sky was back. His eyes were the color of the sky.

Shouldn't I be mad at him? she thought dazedly. *Whose dumb idea was it to walk on the avalanche trail?*

"We've got to move on if you can," Bruce said, turning away. "We're losing daylight."

Lila shook snow from her hair. "I'm ready when you are." She wanted to get away from this place of gleaming fresh snow and near death, even if her knees weren't completely steady.

Bruce walked ahead of her, breaking a path through the heavy melting snow under the trees.

"I'm sorry I said we should walk in the clear," he said. "I guess it should have hit me *why* it was clear."

Lila looked at his back in astonishment. *I bet this is the first time Bruce Patman apologized for anything in his life.*

"Thanks for yelling and saving me," he went on.

"Well, um, thanks for pulling me out," Lila said.

Somehow it isn't exactly a fair exchange, though, she thought. *If it weren't for him, I wouldn't even be here.*

"Although you could have figured out we shouldn't be walking there too." Bruce swiped up a handful of snow to drink.

"Your piloting skills *landed* me in front of that avalanche!" Lila snapped. "I'd keep quiet if I were you."

"Oh, chill." Bruce sounded tired. "You couldn't have done any better."

"Couldn't have done any *better*!" Lila shouted. "Would you mind explaining to me how I could have done worse than crashing the plane at the very top of the Sierra Nevada?"

Bruce was silent for a few seconds, tramping through the snow.

"Here—" He held his hand out behind him as he kept walking. "Have a chocolate. I haven't got the energy to fight with you."

Lila swallowed the rest of her angry words. She didn't have the energy to fight with him right then, either. Lila hadn't realized she was starving. She tore into the chocolate.

"So this is how a wild animal eats," she called to Bruce. "Just rip into food with your fangs."

"We'll probably be eating each other before we get out of this," Bruce said. Lila wondered if he was kidding.

Something is happening to us out here, she

thought as she tramped after Bruce. The cold of evening was beginning to settle, and the trees were black fingers against the sky. *Maybe we're turning into animals. No, that's not it—not yet, anyway. Could Bruce be turning into a person?*

"I thought I had an outfit for every occasion, but I was wrong," Jessica muttered, pushing a pile of clothes to one side of her closet. "I don't have anything just right for a burglary."

Jessica rummaged through Elizabeth's dresser drawers. Buried in the middle of Elizabeth's clothes was just what she needed: black leggings and a black T-shirt. Jessica quickly put them on and finished off the outfit with her sister's black flats.

She examined herself in the mirror. Excellent. If it was dark enough, she should blend right into the night. Unfortunately, her golden hair still gleamed. Well, she'd have to hope for the best.

Jessica grabbed open the door to her room. "I can't get this burglary perfect in less than a day," she muttered. If anyone saw her breaking into Professor Martin's office and reported her, she'd just say they'd made a mistake. There were lots of blondes on campus.

As she ran toward the humanities building, Jessica tried to melt into the shadows away from the lighted walkways. Her hands felt icy. *Just get it over with,* she commanded herself.

Looking swiftly around, she skirted the side of

the building and ran to Professor Martin's window. She took Alison's screwdriver out of her shirt pocket and inserted the blade into one of the screws holding on the screen.

The handle of the screwdriver wobbled. Jessica's hands were shaking so much, she dropped it. *Alison gave me a broken screwdriver,* Jessica realized. *This challenge just gets harder and harder.*

"I'll get caught," she whispered. "I'm so afraid."

Jessica straightened her shoulders. *I don't care if you're afraid,* she told herself. *Get this stunt over with. Remember what's at stake.* She bent over and ran her hands through the grass until she found the fallen screwdriver. Holding the blade with both hands, Jessica managed to unscrew the screen.

She lifted herself over the windowsill and dropped to the floor.

The shadowy office was lit only by moonlight glaring through the window. Jessica thought she saw someone in a dark corner.

"Don't be ridiculous," she said softly. "Now, where is that stupid book?"

Jessica flicked on a little flashlight and shone it over the bookcase. The light wavered in her hands, and she could barely read the titles. What if she couldn't find the book? What if Professor Martin had taken it home to read?

Then she saw it. The spidery gold letters

gleamed in the flickering light: *Lord Byron.* Jessica pulled the musty old book out from between the other musty old books and tucked it under her arm.

Something shifted in the corner.

God, there is *somebody in here!* Jessica screamed, but no sound came out of her constricted throat. Tripping over her feet, she turned to run.

Powerful flashlights sprang out of the corner, blinding her.

"Campus security!" a voice yelled. "Freeze!"

"OK, the coast is clear!" Billie hissed, flinging open the closet door. "My parents are drinking coffee in the kitchen. You can sneak around the edge of the living room and get out to Mike's."

Steven crouched in the closet, blinking in the light. He tried to stand, but his feet and most of his legs were asleep from being crammed into the small space.

Billie hauled him up. She handed him his suitcase.

"How's it going?" Steven whispered.

"Awful." Billie smiled wanly. "I was afraid you were going to sneeze or something and give away the show. I don't want my parents to catch us now—I'll look like such a liar. To say nothing of an idiot."

"We'll get through this." Steven leaned over and kissed her cheek. He almost fell; his feet still felt as if they weren't quite part of his body.

"I'm sorry I stuffed you in the closet," she whispered.

"It's OK. I'll call you," Steven whispered back.

Steven tiptoed across the living room. He caught a glimpse of the Winklers sitting with their backs to him at the kitchen table.

"Billie, could we have some more of this delicious coffee, please?" Mr. Winkler called. "And you'd better call the landlord about getting an exterminator. I heard thumps in the bedroom. Sounds like you've got rats. Big ones."

Steven's half-asleep ankle gave out, and he lost his balance. His suitcase swung into the wall with a resounding *boom*.

"Better check the living room too," Mr. Winkler added.

Nina opened the door to her dorm room. Bryan stood there, holding out one delicate, long-stemmed orange tiger lily.

She remembered telling him that it was her favorite flower. Nina took the lily and stroked its delicate black-spotted petals.

"Friends?" he asked.

Nina kept looking at the flower. How could she tell him what she'd decided?

"Can I come in?" Bryan asked, leaning over to look into her face.

Nina melted a little at his smile. "OK." She put

the flower into a glass of water on her nightstand. She didn't know what to say next.

"Let's just forget what happened at the BSU meeting and start over," Bryan blurted.

"Bryan, we need to talk."

"We *are* talking."

"No, you're talking. And not about what we need to talk about." Nina wondered if she was making any sense at all.

Bryan moved closer. "I'd be glad to shut up."

"Bryan, what happened at that meeting was important," Nina said, exasperated even though her heart was pounding. "We think so differently. I know we've ignored that because we're physically attracted to each other—"

"No!" Bryan said in mock amazement. "I think you're a very ugly young woman. But irresistible."

"Be serious."

"All right." Bryan fell back onto her bed and looked up at her. "What do you think we should do?"

"Break up," Nina said. She was glad that her voice wobbled only a little. She'd stayed awake most of last night until she was sure of this decision.

"Why?" Bryan asked. He leaned back on his elbows and stared at Nina, his mouth slightly agape.

I'll bet not many girls have broken up with him, Nina thought, looking at his muscular, tall body sprawled on her bed. "For one thing, you're pig-headed. For another, we're too different. We're like protons and electrons—opposites," she said, her voice flat.

"According to my memories of high-school chemistry, in the right situation protons and electrons create a perfect balance." Bryan looked over at Nina, his expression expectant.

"You get my point," she responded weakly.

Bryan stood and walked around the room. "I don't like it, but if that's what you really want, I guess I don't have much choice."

Nina closed her eyes. She felt a little faint. *Of course that's not what I really want*, she screamed silently.

Then she felt Bryan kissing her softly on her throat, all the way down to the top of her loose cotton blouse. He nibbled along her jawline; then his mouth came down on hers. Nina parted her lips for a slow, delicious kiss.

After what seemed like an hour, Nina pulled away.

"Stop," she whispered.

"Right." Bryan's voice was unsteady. He got up and walked to the door. With one foot already in the hallway, he turned around. "I'll see you around, Nina," he said softly.

As she heard the door click shut, tears welled up in Nina's eyes. "Good-bye, Bryan," she whispered aloud. "I love you."

* * *

"Elizabeth, you have to come quick!" Jessica sobbed into the phone.

Now what? Elizabeth thought frantically. She was already peeling off her pajamas with one hand and groping in a drawer for a T-shirt with the other. Couldn't Jessica stay out of trouble for a minute? "Where are you?" she asked. "What's going on?"

"Campus security. I—I can't explain completely what happened until you get here. You won't believe this place. But . . . I got caught taking Professor Martin's stupid book." Jessica hiccuped.

"What book?"

"Some ancient poetry thing."

"Not his Byron." Elizabeth's blood ran cold.

"Yes." Jessica sighed heavily.

"Jessica, do you know how valuable that book is?" Elizabeth cried.

"I do now." Jessica's voice shook. "Oh, Liz, hurry. The security officers are threatening to keep me here all night until they get to the bottom of this. You've got to talk them out of it."

"I'll be over as fast as I can run. Tell them not to do anything until I get there." Elizabeth banged down the phone.

She threw on a pair of jeans, shoved her feet into her running shoes, and rushed out the door. Why had Jessica stolen a signed copy of Byron's poetry at midnight?

"With Jessica you never know," Elizabeth muttered, flying up the steps to the security office. "But I'm sure the story will be good." She flung open the door and gasped.

Half a dozen green-shirted security officers were milling around the room. A couple of two-way radios sputtered and chattered. Jessica sat against a back wall on a metal folding chair, looking very small. A huge, muscular man with a gun in a holster was questioning her.

"I just don't know what you're talking about!" Jessica wailed. "I'm a student here. I've never even *considered* breaking into another professor's office." Jessica's blue-green eyes brimmed over with tears.

"Why did you steal that book?" the officer demanded.

"As a joke," Jessica said faintly.

Everybody in the room was listening closely to the interrogation, Elizabeth saw. She rushed to her twin.

A security officer blocked her. "Hold it," he said. "Where do you think you're going?"

"I need to talk to my sister," Elizabeth practically shouted. She had just noticed a pair of unlocked handcuffs on the table next to Jessica. "You're not going to handcuff her, are you?"

"Not now. But this is serious business." The officer shook his head.

"Who are you?" Elizabeth asked.

"I'm Timothy Simmons. I'm head of campus security."

"Tim? Phone," one of the other officers interrupted.

"Excuse me." Mr. Simmons took the telephone and spoke into it for a moment. Then he waved over Jessica's guard.

Elizabeth darted to her sister's side. "Jessica?" she whispered as soon as she was sure the other security officers weren't listening. "What are the charges? I can't believe security would treat you like this just because you stole a book. What else did you do?"

"Nothing!" Jessica whispered back. "I swear."

"I guess we just have to wait and see what they say," Elizabeth said with a sigh.

"I tried to call Steven, since he's the legal expert, but some woman answered the phone at his apartment and said she couldn't imagine why he'd be there," Jessica said, rubbing tears from her cheeks. "Oh, Liz, I'm losing my mind. Look at those handcuffs. They brought me over from the English building in them. I was so embarrassed. What if somebody saw me?"

"Calm down," Elizabeth said, squeezing her sister's hand. "We'll get this straightened out."

The security chief came over to them, followed by Jessica's guard. "OK," he said to Jessica. "It's not as bad as we thought."

"It's not?" Jessica said weakly.

"Why not?" Elizabeth asked quickly. "What happened?"

"Don't argue, Liz!" Jessica cried. "I'm sure it's still bad enough!"

Mr. Simmons looked at her sternly. "Now we've got to decide what to do with you tonight."

"I'll bail her out, if necessary," Elizabeth said.

The security chief looked at them doubtfully. "We're calling the owner of the book right now. We'll see what he says about what sort of charges he intends to file. I'm not convinced this one isn't a flight risk."

"Of course she's not a flight risk," Elizabeth said firmly. *Just flighty to a distressing degree*, she thought.

Jessica's guard hung up the telephone. "OK," he said to Elizabeth. "That was Professor Martin. We're not releasing the name of your sister until formal charges are pressed, but at our discretion Professor Martin has agreed that she can go free for now."

"How did you know the book was his?" Elizabeth asked. It sounded as if Professor Martin had made the entire campus security force visit his office to admire the book.

"Because it's so valuable," the security officer explained. "We have an inventory of all items of extraordinary value on campus."

"How much is it worth?" Elizabeth asked.

The security officer looked at her sternly. "You

don't really need to know, do you?" he said. He wrote something in a notebook.

Elizabeth closed her eyes. There was no point in telling him that to Jessica the book wasn't worth a ripped powder puff.

"All right, girls, you can go." Mr. Simmons stared hard at them. "But don't leave the area."

"No, of course not. Good night," Elizabeth said, steering a numb Jessica to the door.

"I just want to go home and sleep and wake up in the morning and find out this is a nightmare," Jessica said with a groan as soon as they were outside.

"Jessica, you must have lost your mind," Elizabeth said fiercely. "Why on earth did you steal that book?"

"I can't tell you," Jessica said. "I can't tell anybody."

"Jessica!" Isabella cried, rushing over to hug her. Elizabeth saw that most of the Theta membership had surrounded the security building.

"Oh, I get it now," Elizabeth said in disgust. "They put you up to this, didn't they, Jess? I should have known."

Jessica didn't seem to hear the question.

Elizabeth sighed. She didn't like the Thetas, and she knew the feeling was mutual. The Thetas had formed an Elizabeth Wakefield hate club after she'd made it clear what she thought of the Thetas' snotty ways during sorority rush week last semester.

"Jessica, let's call it a night."

"I changed my mind about going home, Liz." Jessica blew her nose. "I want to stay for a while. I need my friends' support."

"Well, you sure got a lot of it—fast. How'd you know Jessica was here?" Elizabeth asked Denise Waters.

"Alison told us Jess had been caught. I don't know how she knew—someone must have called her," Denise answered.

"I notice your fearless vice president isn't here now. Jessica, come on. We've got to call a lawyer."

"Let's wait till tomorrow. This could all blow over by then," Jessica said. "With a little help from our friends."

"Jessica!" Elizabeth tugged her arm.

"Stop it, Liz!" Jessica pulled away. "I've had a terrible night. I've probably got a concussion from security's pushing me into the wall of Martin's office. I'm just not up to dealing with this now."

"You have to deal with it. You're in a lot of trouble," Elizabeth warned. "I know Professor Martin pretty well, and he's not going to be happy about this, to say the least. . . ."

"Liz, you could talk to him, couldn't you?" Jessica turned enormous, serious blue eyes on her.

"I don't want to," Elizabeth said in exasperation. "He's going to think I'm a jerk too. What would I say to him? 'My twin sister stole your most valuable possession. I don't know why, but it had something to do with the Thetas. I think they wanted to flush it down the toilet.' "

"We weren't going to harm a single page." Jessica glared at her.

"Let's go to the coffeehouse, Jess," Isabella said, putting an arm around her shoulders. "We'll talk this over and soothe your nerves."

"That's what I need," Jessica said, giving Elizabeth an injured look.

"All right, Jessica." Elizabeth frowned back. "You know perfectly well what you're doing, as usual. I'm not going to lose sleep over this if you're not."

"I won't be late—but don't wait up." Jessica tossed back her hair.

"It's already late," Elizabeth said, but Jessica was walking away under a row of palm trees with her Theta friends.

Jessica doesn't realize how serious this is, Elizabeth said to herself as she walked slowly back to the dorm. *But she will.*

Chapter Seven

"You took a big chance coming here," Celine hissed, looking up and down the hall to her apartment. At least he'd waited until night—a cloudy, thick black night when high clouds covered the moon and stars. She wasn't really surprised to see him.

William shrugged and pushed by her through the doorway. "Invite me in, Celine," he said over his shoulder.

Celine frowned and leaned against the doorjamb. He certainly wasn't acting overjoyed to be in her company.

"This is a terrible apartment," William said coldly, stroking his long, pale hair out of his eyes. He walked to the tiny window overlooking the street, lit a cigarette, and looked back at her, smiling ironically.

Celine gazed at her tiny apartment. It was only

one room and a bath, with the kitchen things in an alcove. She tried to look at her drab furnishings through William's eyes. In particular she noted the two secondhand chairs with stuffing leaking out of rips in the seats—those were an anonymous gift from the last person stuck living there. She couldn't even imagine what her Granny Boudreaux would say about this fleabag. It *was* terrible.

Celine opened her mouth to ask William if the nuthouse was a nicer place. But something about his ice-cold blue eyes wouldn't let her.

"You shouldn't come here unless I say the coast is clear," Celine chided, going to the kitchen to put on the espresso pot. Celine carefully lifted her best cups out of the cabinet. She was a little afraid to have William in the apartment. It was probably a crime.

But her life had been so dull lately, that was a crime too. That was why she was happy William was back. Celine loaded a tray with the two cups of espresso and went back out to the living room.

William still stood in front of the window, smoking. He looked as exquisitely handsome as ever. Celine longed to get his attention. "A penny for your thoughts, William." She set the tray down on the coffee table.

William whirled. His eyes blazed, and his face twisted grotesquely.

"Revenge," he said hoarsely. "Revenge is *sweet.*

So sweet," he muttered, turning to the window again.

Celine gulped. He seemed absolutely insane.

Then she smiled. "Honey, I know what you're talking about. But if you so much as go *near* Elizabeth Wakefield, the cops and the FBI are going to be all over you like ducks on a june bug."

"I know." William's lips twitched. "That's why I've got you." He sat on the couch and reached for an espresso.

Celine stared at him thoughtfully. She sat down next to him, hard enough to jog his coffee. What was she going to get out of this? William had better show some gratitude, starting tonight.

"So, Celine," William said smoothly, "I've got some ideas about entertaining Elizabeth."

I hate the way he says "Elizabeth," Celine thought, lounging back on the couch. *His voice drops low, and he sort of strokes her name with his tongue.* Why didn't William's voice drop and stroke her name?

"Like what?" Celine drawled. She sat up and ran her fingers along his arm.

William caught her hand as it slid up his arm. For an instant Celine thought he was going to throw it off. Then he brought it to his lips and kissed her fingers. "I'll tell you tomorrow night. Meet me at Sandoval's at eight o'clock."

"That's fifty miles away!" Celine protested.

"It's also a five-star restaurant. I'd like to entertain you too. Much more nicely than I've entertained Elizabeth." William still held her hand.

"I think I might know just how to help you," Celine purred.

Someone banged loudly on the door. That had to be Paul—he was turning into more of a pest every day. Celine gave an exasperated sigh.

"Is that your boyfriend?" William asked with a laugh.

"Not at all." Celine glared at the door. "Just some admirer who's wildly in love with me and can't live without me for a second."

"I was about to leave anyway," William said, rising.

Just when it was getting good, Celine thought. *Damn Paul.* "There's only one door," she pointed out.

"Fire escape." William walked to the window. "I noticed I could get out this way when I came in."

Celine stared in astonishment as William slid out the window into the night. Then she saw his ghostly face still hovering at the window.

"Hey, Celine," he called softly.

"What?"

"Remember—I'm watching you."

Celine felt the hairs on the back of her neck stand up. *I wonder*, she thought. *Is that a promise or a threat?*

* * *

Lila crouched in a clear spot under a tree and struck a match. Darkness closed in on them.

Bruce glanced at Lila. The small circle of light from the match briefly lit up her pretty face. The fire caught the tinder and crackled briskly.

"Where'd you learn to make a fire?" he asked.

"Any pilot is supposed to know elementary first aid and survival tactics," Lila said dryly. She was silent for a minute, watching the fire blaze.

Bruce frowned. "Well, I've only had my pilot's license for a couple of months. And I've never flown in the mountains before."

Lila shrugged and kept staring into the fire.

Why was he bothering to explain himself to her? He looked at her face again in the orange light. The flames lit up its soft oval shape and the curve of her lips. Her expression was somber.

"What are you thinking?" he asked.

"About when we crashed." Lila put out her hands and rubbed them over the fire. "Did you really think I was dead when you left me in the plane?"

"Yeah. I already told you that. I mean, you *looked* dead." What was her point?

"But didn't you even think to make sure? What if I'd been dying?"

"Well, you weren't," Bruce said, reaching behind her for a package of trail mix. "Besides, you left me for dead behind the rocks."

"That was because I couldn't stand it." Lila shifted uncomfortably. "I mean, you know, the blood."

Bruce looked at her for a moment. "I'm not sure I really thought you were dead. I *was* going to come back. But why should I have worried about you? You've got as many lives as a cat."

Lila smiled. "I wonder which life I'm on."

"First there was Lila Fowler, daddy's little rich girl in Sweet Valley." Bruce ticked his finger. "Then Italy, when you married that count. And now after."

"You skipped one life," Lila said, rubbing her calves. "After Italy there was my life at SVU. And now there's my life here, wherever here is." Lila gazed into the wilderness outside the small circle of firelight.

A three-quarter moon was rising to the east, casting a dull blue-white light on the distant mountains. Lila sighed, cupping her face in her hands. Bruce couldn't stop looking at her.

"What's the matter?" Lila asked.

"Maybe you are in another life out here. You look different," he said.

"I can just imagine." Lila sighed. She touched her hair. "My hair has gone natural."

Lila's hair was streaked gold by the sun, and her tanned face glowed. *If she wasn't so temperamental and irritating, she wouldn't be half bad,* Bruce thought. "You don't so look terrible," he said.

"Don't kill me with compliments." Lila was watching the moon rise higher, outlining the tops of the pines with a subdued white gleam. A cold breeze moaned softly through the forest and around the rocks. "Maybe I am different," she said, turning to look at him. "Being out here isn't like college. We're just so alone. . . . I mean, isn't it weird? Who would have imagined the two of us all alone with each other in the mountains? We may never see another person for the rest of our lives, however long that is. Or isn't."

Bruce shivered. "Don't you think we're going to get out of this?" he asked.

Lila looked a little uncertain. "We're making good progress. Do you think we'll make it?"

"Yeah. I mean, sure." Bruce stretched out next to the fire.

Lila unrolled her blanket and small flight pillow and arranged them next to the fire.

Bruce lay down a couple of feet away. He was almost immediately cold from the frozen ground seeping through his thin blanket. His wrist throbbed.

What if a storm hit and they froze? What if his wrist developed gangrene and he lost his hand? What if they just wandered until they starved to death?

Bruce turned on his back and stared at the sky. The stars were very bright and close. They hung like crystals in the sky.

A wolf howl, distant and faint, echoed across the mountain. Another wolf called back.

"Hey, Lila?" Bruce rolled closer to her.

"Yes?" Her back was to him.

"I'm glad you're not dead."

"Here's your bed, Steven." Mike was pointing at the black leather couch in his living room. "Sleep tight."

Steven sighed. It had only been a couple of hours since he'd seen Billie, and already he missed her. Mike was a friend, but he was far from the ideal roommate. Mike's idea of a quiet evening at home included blasting rock music at a volume the whole block could hear.

Steven dropped onto the couch and rested his head on the arm. It was too late to call Billie. But if he didn't, she might think he'd forgotten about her.

Steven looked thoughtfully at the ceiling. Their apartment was directly above Mike's. Steven got up and brought a broom from the utility closet back into the living room. "If I'd thought of this earlier, we could have worked out a code," he said to himself.

Steven lifted the broom and pounded softly on the ceiling. *Nothing. She must be sound asleep.*

Then the ceiling banged back. Steven smiled. "Good night, sweetheart," he said, raising his voice. "Wish I was there."

There was a silence. "Good night," called Billie's parents.

"My book could have been ruined." Professor Martin shook his head and looked at Elizabeth. His black eyes snapped sparks.

Elizabeth fidgeted in her chair. The trouble was, she agreed with him—she thought the Thetas might have been planning to ruin the book too. What else would they do with it? But she wasn't there to tell Professor Martin that.

He's really angry, she said to herself. *It's not going to be easy to get Jessica out of this.*

Not that Jessica cared. She'd come home from Theta House at three in the morning, singing. Elizabeth had no idea what Jessica was singing about. *Why should Jessica worry about anything?* she thought sourly. *She knew I'd try to get her out of this mess somehow.*

"The book's OK, isn't it?" Elizabeth asked. It couldn't hurt to remind him of that.

"Yes. Security caught the thief coming out of my office before she had time to do any real damage." Professor Martin leaned against a bookcase and folded his arms.

Elizabeth tried to think of a new tack. He looked as easy to persuade as granite.

"Well, since you got the book back, no harm was really done," she said cautiously.

"That's not the point. If the thief hadn't

been caught, the book would have been gone forever. I'm sorry, Elizabeth." Professor Martin gave her a half-smile. "I don't want to act like this—vengeful and angry. Especially in front of you. I wish I could dismiss this robbery as a harmless prank. But it wasn't. That young woman almost destroyed an irreplaceable work of art."

Elizabeth couldn't think what more to say. *I can't argue with anything he's said. I could have made that speech.*

"So I'm going to press charges," he went on.

"No, you can't!" Elizabeth cried.

Professor Martin smiled. "You're too soft-hearted, Elizabeth. It's an admirable quality, but your concern is misplaced this time."

What can I do? Elizabeth thought wildly. *He's not taking me seriously.*

"I'm glad you dropped by." His voice was gentle. "I wanted to assign you some reading for our Byron project. I actually almost called you last night to ask you to meet me here. Imagine, we might have surprised the robber."

"I wish we had," Elizabeth said weakly.

"I thought of giving you a key to the office so that you could work here on your own. But now I wonder if that would be safe."

"I'm pretty sure it would be," Elizabeth said.

"I don't want to be responsible for anything happening to my best student." Professor Martin's gaze was warm. "I think we should work together nights."

Jessica collapsed onto a Victorian sofa in the living room at Theta House. She dropped her head onto one of the sofa's puffy arms. She hoped that morning's emergency Theta meeting would be short—she was beat.

Jessica closed her eyes. The room smelled soothingly of old, well-oiled wood. She felt better just being there.

The Thetas will get me out of this jam, she said to herself. *They had to have planned for the possibility that I would get caught.*

The Theta sisters filed into the room and took seats in various chairs and couches. No one said anything. All the faces were gloomy.

The mood has definitely changed from last night, Jessica thought. *It's gotten ugly.* She sat up on the couch and nervously ran her hands through her hair.

Alison Quinn walked briskly into the room and sat on the other end of the sofa from Jessica. She smiled. Jessica didn't smile back.

"*How* could you be so stupid?" Alison demanded suddenly. Her loud voice rang off the walls. "I mean, *really,* Jessica. We ask you to do the simplest thing, and you get caught and put the entire sorority at risk."

Jessica put a hand to her now aching head.

"How did I put the sorority at risk?" Jessica asked, trying to keep her voice steady.

"You can't blame Jessica for something we asked her to do," Isabella cut in, stepping forward.

"Don't play games, Jessica." Alison's face was smooth and cold. She ignored Isabella completely. "We certainly can't tell the authorities that this sorority house sponsored a *theft*. The security office called this morning and asked if you were a Theta sister. I said absolutely not."

Jessica lifted her chin. Exhausted or not, she was going to defend herself. Did Alison think she could just walk over her? "This isn't fair, Alison. I didn't expect the Thetas to *attack* me for doing what you told me to. I was showing my loyalty to the house."

Alison was shaking her head. "And now we're showing our loyalty to the house by trying to protect it after your botched job. There's only one way to handle this situation. Jessica, we're going to have to banish you from the sorority until everything is cleared up."

"That's too severe, Alison." Denise pushed off the wall and looked Alison straight in the eye.

"Believe me, Denise, nothing could hurt me more." Alison put a hand on her heart. "But do you know what could happen if the school finds out about this? We could have our charter revoked."

Denise opened her mouth, then shrugged.

"Alison is right." Magda Helperin, the reserved Theta president, looked at Jessica sympathetically. "I'm sorry, Jessica. We should have thought this through before we asked you to do it. But now—"

"Now we want you to leave this house," Alison interrupted. "No contact with any of the Theta sisters until you're cleared of the crime. While you're trying to clear your name, don't tell the authorities the sorority had anything to do with the break-in. Or you'll never be a Theta."

Jessica swallowed. She couldn't fight back. It was true the Thetas could get into real trouble over this. And she must have done something dumb that tipped off security.

But she had never felt so betrayed.

"Jessica, we'll do everything we can to help, behind the scenes," Denise said quickly.

Jessica nodded numbly.

"Of course we all will," Magda said. "It's the very least we can do."

"This meeting is adjourned," Alison said, clapping once. "Out, Jessica. Nobody talk to her."

Magda looked sharply at Alison but then just said, "No one is to spread this story around. Code of honor." Then she turned on her heel and walked out of the room.

Jessica's heart sank. What would she do if she couldn't clear herself of the crime and the Thetas didn't accept her? James might even dump her when he found out she was a Theta reject.

Jessica walked slowly out of the sorority. Her face was still flushed with humiliation.

She didn't have any support except Isabella and maybe Denise. Where was Lila, her very best friend, when Jessica needed her? Off carousing at a spa, probably splashing in a hot tub with some gorgeous man.

"Jessica!" James's smooth baritone was close behind her.

Jessica turned around, conscious of her bloodshot eyes and rumpled hair.

"What happened?" he asked, looking concerned. "You look like your best friend just died."

Jessica looked at him. The sunlight caught deep auburn lights in his dark hair. His smiling green eyes were the color of a forest pool.

"I guess I'm not in the best mood. I just had kind of an argument with the Thetas at a brunch. I can't talk about it, though." Her smile vanished.

James frowned slightly. "I wish they wouldn't hassle you. I thought Sigma had squared them away on that." His face brightened. "I know what you need after a difficult morning." James took her arm and pulled her around 180 degrees. "Let's go to the beach. I'll surf a little, and we'll sit on a big blanket with a picnic and talk."

"Don't we have classes this morning?" Jessica laughed.

"Yeah, California Sunshine one-oh-one." James took a firm hold of Jessica's elbow and steered her toward the parking lot where he kept his red Mazda Miata.

"I just love higher learning," Jessica said. Already she could feel the morning's tension draining away. *I hope that while I'm at the beach, Liz is doing something worthwhile—like figuring out how I can put this nightmare behind me!*

Chapter Eight

Lila rubbed her face and neck with snow. "I might as well look decent for whoever finds my body," she muttered.

The morning light spilled through the valleys below. The fiercely blue sky gripped the dark-green pines and snowy slopes like a hand.

Lila almost smiled. The beauty of this place was so raw and untamed. She rubbed the lump on her head. It was smaller, and she felt energetic.

Bruce was standing under a massive pine tree, consulting a compass. Lila was surprised to see him looking so comfortable in the wilderness.

"Hey, I didn't know you had that." Lila walked over to him. "We might be able to use it. Although I guess all we really have to do is keep walking downhill."

"Follow me," Bruce said confidently. "You ready?"

"Yep." Lila stuffed her blanket and pillow into his knapsack and walked behind him.

"Look at that!" Bruce said a few minutes later. He pointed ahead.

A huge meadow stretched before them. The snow had melted from it, and small lakes, the topaz color of the sky, dotted the long brown grass.

"It's absolutely beautiful," Lila said.

She began to run. The clean, fresh air blew on her cheeks. She whirled to face Bruce, her eyes sparkling.

"Tag?" Bruce yelled, racing after her. "I'm it!"

Lila fled around a pool. It reflected the tall grasses growing around it, and fast-moving little white clouds.

Bruce paused on the other side, panting. "I could wade across and get you," he said.

"Try it!" Lila said, laughing. "You'll just get wet feet."

He took one step toward her and grimaced. "Help! Hey, this isn't funny, Lila! Something's got me under the water!"

Lila rushed around the pool. "What is it? Is it biting you? Give me your hand!" God, how would she get Bruce out of there if he lost a leg?

She could hardly grab his hand, he was thrashing so much. He seemed to be in agony. Lila was terrified. What lived in these lakes?

She caught hold of his wrist . . . and Bruce

yanked her toward him, hard. "You're it!" he shouted. "Boy, did you fall for that! Dork!"

"Oh, you . . . pond creature!" Lila stared at him for a second, angry. Then she laughed. She seized his wrist in both hands and pulled.

They fell back on the grassy bank side by side. Bruce grinned at her.

Lila grinned back.

A cloud covered the sun. Lila shivered. She'd gotten splashed in the water battle.

Bruce still held her hand.

"We'd better walk some more," she said. "We really need to keep pushing."

"Yeah." Bruce let go of her and stood. He got out his compass and checked it. "OK," he said. "We'll head due south."

Lila tramped after him. She munched some trail mix. *That was fun,* she thought. *I actually had fun with Bruce Patman. This mountain air must be getting to me.*

They crossed the meadow easily. Without snow their pace was almost doubled.

Then it got harder. The snow was back on the hills. "Bruce—" Lila caught up to him. "Why are we walking uphill?"

"Because the compass says to."

"But—"

"Lila, stop arguing with me," Bruce said impatiently. "This is a scientific instrument. It can't be wrong."

They walked on for what seemed like miles, struggling through the snow, clawing aside underbrush. The sun began to drop in the sky. Lila's feet felt almost too heavy to lift.

Suddenly the terrain looked terrifyingly familiar.

It couldn't be. It absolutely was impossible. But . . .

They were back at the upside-down, shattered plane. The plane of death.

Lila stared at it in utter disbelief. "No," she said. *"No! Even you couldn't do something this dumb!"*

"Just shut up!" Bruce shouted.

Lila sank to the ground. "You're a total idiot," she said, sobbing with rage. "How could you get us this lost?"

"Get off my case!" Bruce ripped off his backpack. "I'm sick of you laying into me!"

"Oh, I guess I should just smile and say, 'That's OK, Bruce, let's walk around the plane another fifty times for fun,'" Lila screamed. "I should have known not to trust an imbecile who already got us lost hundreds of miles out in the wilderness!"

Bruce started for her, fists clenched.

Then he seemed to get ahold of himself.

"Excuse me for not being Mr. Perfect," he said icily.

"Let's make camp." Lila got up and turned her

back on him. "In the morning *I'll* figure out what to do. From now on we're going to do exactly what *I* say."

Bruce didn't answer. He threw himself to the ground next to their old campfire site and put his head in his hands.

Lila tossed some sticks on the site and made a small fire. Then she lay down next to the fire, as far from Bruce as possible.

Tears ran down her cheeks. *Why did I ever trust him?* she thought. *I'm as stupid as he is. I'm going to die next to the wreck of that plane.*

Lila fell into a restless sleep. She dreamed she was following Bruce through endless miles of snow. They traipsed on and on. *No!* Lila screamed. *We're back at the plane!* She lost the plane in a blizzard that suddenly started to fall.

Lila woke, cold with sweat. She was completely disoriented. She sat up, pushing back her hair. *Something's different*, she said to herself. And then she realized—Bruce was gone.

Nina walked straight by the palm tree Bryan was sitting under.

"Oh, come on, Nina. You can at least say hi," Bryan said reasonably.

"Hi." Nina had tried to sneak by only so that he wouldn't see how upset she was. Although she knew she'd made the right decision about their breaking up, she couldn't sleep after he'd left the night before. Or study. Or even eat much. Nina had never had a problem with her appetite before. She was in serious trouble over this man.

"Sit for a while," Bryan said. "Enjoy the afternoon."

Nina squinted at the sky. Small, puffy white clouds lined up at the horizon like a train. The sun was beating down on her head. "I can only stay for a minute," she told him, sitting on the grass a safe distance away. "I've got physics."

"Always physics." Bryan shook his head.

"Always politics," Nina shot back. "At least I learned something about politics from you. You never learned anything from me."

Bryan threw up his hands. "I'm not good at science, Nina."

"Well, you do have other talents," Nina said grudgingly.

Bryan was looking at her lips.

"I was thinking that you're a good organizer." Nina tried to sound stern. He looked so incredibly gorgeous, leaning against the palm tree with his long legs sprawled in front of him.

"Thank you." Bryan rolled off the tree onto his side.

"I could never run a meeting," Nina said, stretching out next to him. Her hands were sweating a little, but it was a warm day. "I think it's wonderful that you can. But I guess that just proves my point. . . . We don't have much . . . in common."

He was slowly wiggling toward her over the short space of grass separating them.

"I guess we don't," Bryan said huskily.

His mouth was so close . . . his arms were around her, pressing her to him.

The sun danced behind her closed eyelids. "Go get 'em, Bryan!" somebody yelled from the path, and whistled. Nina pushed Bryan away.

"It's barely noon," she gasped. She tried to straighten out her clothes, but it was hard to rearrange them while she was sitting down. "We can't do this all the time."

"Why not?"

"Because . . ." Nina couldn't think of one concrete reason.

Bryan tugged her back down and kissed her hard.

Nina gave up and kissed him back.

"I'm glad we're friends again," he said sincerely.

Nina dropped her arms. "We're *not* friends."

"We seemed like friends a second ago." Bryan was giving her that open, hopeful, determined look that she always fell for.

"Friends can talk to each other," Nina said firmly.

"We talk, but we're on different wavelengths. Speaking of which—" Bryan tapped his watch.

Does he want me to go? Nina thought. *I'm not*

sure I can solve equations when my hands are sweating and I'm out of breath like this.

But she did have class. She got up and brushed off her jeans.

Bryan's hazel eyes were serious as he looked up at her. "Hey, Nina . . ."

"What?" She tried not to look at him.

"There's a BSU meeting this afternoon at two. Give me one more chance, at least there. I'd like you to hear what I plan to say." Bryan's hazel eyes held hers. "It might surprise you."

"Thanks for stopping by on such short notice," Professor Martin said.

"I was glad to." Elizabeth set her notebook on the edge of his desk and sat across from him. She was more than glad to be there. *Now all I need to do is figure out a way to bring up the robbery again without making him mad,* she thought, returning his smile.

"I had an inspiration," he said.

Elizabeth looked interested.

Professor Martin picked up a paperback poetry anthology from his desk. Elizabeth noticed that the old copy of Byron was gone from the shelf.

Professor Martin leafed through the pages and began to read.

> *"She walks in beauty, like the night*
> *Of cloudless climes and starry skies;*

And all that's best of dark and bright
Meet in her aspect and her eyes:
Thus mellow'd to that tender light
Which heaven to gaudy day denies."

"You read beautifully," Elizabeth said admiringly.

"Thank you." He dropped the book onto the desk and rolled his chair around beside hers. "My inspiration is this. For our project we could compare Byron's earlier love poems to his later ones. My initial reaction, when I was reading the poems, is that Byron became much more cynical in his later writings. What do you think?"

His chair seemed a little close to hers. Elizabeth remembered her fantasy of walking in English gardens with him. Only this time they were discussing Byron as they walked along a path arched with pink primroses, bordered by manicured, bright-green lawns.

She tried to focus her thoughts. "I think it sounds wonderful. But Byron wrote so many love poems, it'll be quite a project to analyze them all."

"Let's make the time," the professor said, smiling. "Since it's something we're both interested in."

"All right," Elizabeth said, feeling more like a valued colleague than a student.

"Do you have a complete edition of Byron? If not, you can borrow this one." He reached for the paperback copy on his desk.

"A new Byron," she said. "What happened to the old one?"

Professor Martin groaned. "Let's not talk about that again. I thought about what you said this morning. I agree with you that no harm was done, but it's not worth anguishing about. I'm going to press charges and be done with it. Let's read some more Byron."

I'd love to, Elizabeth said to herself, *but I have to make you talk about the robbery.*

"I really think it was just a tasteless joke," she said cautiously. At some point he might bite her head off.

"Elizabeth?" Professor Martin said pleadingly. "Can we drop this?"

If I tell him Jessica is my sister, he'll understand why I want to keep talking about it, Elizabeth thought.

Professor Martin was bent over the paperback Byron.

Elizabeth sighed. It was obvious that he considered the subject closed.

> *"The smiles that win, the tints that glow,*
> *But tell of days in goodness spent,*
> *A mind at peace with all below,*
> *A heart whose love is innocent!"*

Professor Martin read. He glanced at her. "It's lovely, isn't it?"

There was something about the way he was

looking at her. . . . Elizabeth wondered what he was thinking.

"Byron's poetic technique is great," she said carefully. Then she remembered. Tom and Jessica! Elizabeth checked her watch. She was supposed to meet them for coffee and then go with Tom to the station for a last edit of the Sigma cheating story.

She got up hastily and grabbed her notebook. "I'm sorry, but I've got to run," she said. "I completely forgot some work I have to do at the station."

Elizabeth turned to go.

Professor Martin stood between her and the door.

Elizabeth stepped closer to him. He didn't move.

Then he smiled. "I'll walk you out."

Jessica almost ran to the coffeehouse to meet Elizabeth. It would feel good to dump her problems onto her sister.

Elizabeth was sipping cappuccino in a booth near the far window. To Jessica's annoyance Tom Watts was at her side.

"Liz!" Jessica waved and rushed over to join her. Elizabeth was smiling and talking to Tom, her blond head close to his dark one. "Did you talk to Professor Martin?" Jessica asked breathlessly, pulling up a chair.

Elizabeth's face fell. "I tried," she said. "Twice.

He said he's going to press charges, Jessica, and he means it. I don't think anything I say will change his mind."

Jessica sighed. "What did you say to him?" Tom was irritating her even more than usual. She wished he would go away for a few minutes so that she and Elizabeth could have a private conversation. But he just sat there, like Elizabeth's brand-new Siamese twin.

"Everything I could think of." Elizabeth shrugged. "Professor Martin and I have gotten pretty close, working on this research project together, but it didn't make any difference."

"What happened to you really sucks, Jessica." Tom's dark eyes were thoughtful. "I was in a fraternity for a long time. . . ."

I really hope you're going to tell me all about it, Jessica thought, leaning on her elbows and sighing loudly.

"The whole idea of a sorority or fraternity is that the members stick together when the going gets tough," Tom went on.

"Who said the Thetas had anything to do with this?" Jessica cut in. "But I'm just a pledge, so what happens to me doesn't matter so much."

"Yeah," Tom said. "You're not in on their discussions. I wonder if there's something going on you don't know about."

This was really getting ridiculous. Jessica had to sit there listening to Tom's stupid advice while her life was being sucked rapidly down a toilet. "Liz, you weren't supposed to tell him about this," Jessica began, but she shut herself up. What was the use? Elizabeth told Tom everything.

If only he would go somewhere and stop interfering.

Tom got up.

"The power of positive thinking," Jessica muttered.

"I've got to meet the guys for a pickup basketball game," he said. "See you later, sweetie." He kissed Elizabeth's cheek.

Jessica stopped herself just in time from sticking a finger down her throat.

Elizabeth was silent for a minute, watching Tom stride toward the coffeehouse door. "Jessica, what are you going to do?" she finally said. "I'm out of ideas."

"So am I," Jessica said sadly. "The Thetas aren't going to help me get out of this."

Elizabeth looked furious. "Why not? This was all their idea, wasn't it?"

"Sort of. But don't tell anyone. Anyone *else,*" Jessica said pointedly. "Obviously you already told Tom."

"Why are *you* protecting the Thetas? They couldn't care less what happens to you," Elizabeth said with annoyance.

"Because I still want to join the sorority. Look, Liz, even if I tried to blame them, it wouldn't help. They'll just say they didn't have anything to do with it. It'll be my word against theirs."

Elizabeth screwed up her face. "I'll never understand why you want to be around those people."

"I just can't tell on them." Jessica tossed back her hair. "I guess all I can do now is keep hoping for the best."

"That hasn't worked very well so far." Elizabeth leaned across the table. "Jessica, if Professor Martin heard the true story about the robbery, he might change his mind about pressing charges."

Elizabeth sat back.

"We can't do it that way," Jessica insisted. "Go talk to him again. I'm sure there's some angle you haven't tried."

"There isn't," Elizabeth said.

Elizabeth leaned back in her chair in the WSVU newsroom and glanced at the replay of Tom's segment on the cheating at Sigma. "Good work," she said to him.

"You don't seem too excited," Tom said reproachfully, sitting down beside her.

"Sorry." Elizabeth gave him a half-smile. "It's all this trouble with Jessica. I can't get my mind off it. I probably should have been able to help her with Professor Martin. I do have a special relationship with him."

"Yeah, I guess you do."

Tom's voice sounded funny. Elizabeth

looked at him in surprise. "What?" she asked.

"Nothing." Tom shrugged. "I just wish you were as excited about our new story as you are about your project with that professor."

"Maybe I'm just not excited about digging up everybody's dirt. Lately, it seems like the only interesting news is bad news." Elizabeth looked into Tom's dark eyes, trying to read his thoughts.

Tom's fingers traced a curve from her ear to her collarbone. "You're always interesting," he said softly.

Elizabeth stroked his hair back from his forehead and touched her lips to his.

Tom wouldn't let her stop at that. He half rose out of his chair, covering her body with his, and pressed his mouth down on hers.

"I can think of more comfortable places we could go," he murmured. "Maybe my room, or yours. Anybody's room." He got up and walked over to his computer to switch it off. For a moment he stood there reading the screen.

Tom dumped the cover onto his computer and turned to her with a smile. "My room, yours, or somewhere in between?" he asked.

Elizabeth smiled back uncertainly. "Let's start walking," she said.

Why do I keep comparing Tom and Professor Martin? she thought as she followed Tom out of the newsroom. It wasn't as if Professor Martin could ever be her boyfriend.

Chapter Nine

There's no way to get comfortable with a broken arm, Winston thought, moving his injured limb to a new position on the pillows. The arm was frozen in an L-shaped white plaster cast.

Winston groaned under his breath. How was he supposed to get any sleep with this thing?

Anoushka, one of Winston's hallmates, opened the door to his dorm room and peeked in. "Poor Winnie!" she cried. "You look awful! Does it hurt?"

"Only when someone asks me if it hurts," Winston said peevishly. Winston noticed that his accident had brought out the maternal instincts of the two hundred women who lived with him in this all-female dorm. Girls had been cooing and clucking over him from the moment Denise had brought him home from the hospital.

Winston sighed. He felt completely humiliated.

It seemed as if everyone on campus had gathered yesterday morning to watch him being scraped off the tree and loaded into the ambulance.

"Look at all your stuff," Anoushka said, picking up some of the get-well gifts on Winston's desk. "Who brought all this junk? Horror novels, chocolates, workout videos . . ."

"I'm a god," Winston said. "Whoever does not appease me with offerings will be sacrificed."

A knock sounded at the door. "Come in," Winston called. *More presents?* he wondered.

Two very attractive heads looked in: Maia's and Candy's. More hallmates.

"We heard rumors you have food," Candy said.

"Feast, my subjects," Winston said, waving his good arm at the spread.

The two women looked at each other and made faces. "Win, you have delusions of grandeur," Maia said with a snort.

"And chocolates to feed to anybody who sucks up," Winston said loftily.

Denise knocked on the open door and rushed in. "I'm sorry I left you alone for so long," she said breathlessly. "I had to do something. How do you feel?"

"I'm OK," Winston said. He was worried about her, though. Tears sparkled in Denise's clear blue eyes.

"Oh, Winnie, I still feel so guilty." Denise wiped her cheeks with her hands. "I should never have made you race on Rollerblades. We should have done something safe, like go bowling."

"No sport is very safe when you do it with me," Winston said, closing his eyes. His arm really hurt. "The last time I bowled, I dropped the ball on my foot and got a strike in someone else's lane. Face it, Denise; life with me is dangerous."

Denise sniffed. Winston opened one eye and saw that she was smiling a little.

"We'll leave you alone now, O Great God Flat-on-His-Butt," Anoushka said, popping a chocolate into her mouth and grabbing Maia's arm. Winston opened both eyes and glared at them. Maia took the chocolate box on her way out.

The pain in his arm stabbed relentlessly. Winston pushed the ache to the back of his mind. He didn't want Denise to realize how much he was hurting and feel bad again.

"Don't worry so much," he said, taking her hand and pulling her down beside him on the bed. "I'm going to make a complete recovery and be as good a Rollerblader as ever—you were there when the doctor told me that. Want to sign my cast?"

Denise wiped her eyes and nodded. She picked out a pink felt tip from the pencil holder on the desk.

Denise held his arm steady and drew a large pink heart in the middle of the cast.

"Do you know how much flak I'm going to get from the guys when I'm walking around with that?" Winston asked. He couldn't have been happier.

"I'm not done yet." Denise carefully wrote in the heart: *D. W. loves W. E.* Then she put an arrow through the heart.

Winston could feel his own heart melting. "Come here," he said, drawing her to him. "How about a one-armed kiss? It'll be like kissing a slot machine."

"Hmm." Denise put her lips to his. "Different, but"—she kissed him again—"nice."

Winston wedged a pillow beneath his head and kissed Denise more deeply. There were advantages to being bedridden, he realized.

Denise pushed herself away from Winston's chest and sat up. "I think you'd better get some sleep, Win—and that's obviously not going to happen with me around."

"You could stay and take a nap with me." Winston couldn't imagine a nicer way to go to sleep than with Denise snuggled up next to him.

"For some reason I don't think the two of us lying on your bed would be conducive to sleep," Denise laughed. "But as soon as you wake up, I'll have a wonderful surprise for you."

Celine tossed her wrap to the coat girl and flounced over to the maître d'. She was nervous, although she hoped she didn't look it. A lot was riding on this dinner with William. She wanted him to say that she was going to be his girlfriend.

"I'm not going to play second fiddle in Elizabeth Wakefield's orchestra anymore," Celine murmured, peering into the dim interior of the restaurant. Candlelight flickered on the tables. "If William doesn't know that now, he will after tonight."

Several of the male patrons were casting admiring glances at Celine's expensively casual gold-macramé dress. William wasn't among them.

"Where is he?" Celine muttered as the maître d' ushered her to a table. "You'd think he'd manage to be on time for our first real date." Well, it was probably a complicated matter to escape from a nuthouse. That wasn't the kind of thing she wanted to dwell on this evening, though.

The maître d' helped her into her chair. At least William still got fantastic service: She was sitting next to a huge window that looked right out on the ocean. She could smell the clean salt spray from the waves crashing and foaming against the black rocks far below.

"The tide is full, the moon lies fair," a deep voice said in her ear.

Celine turned with her most dazzling smile. "Why, William. You're just a little late."

"Sorry. I stopped to buy you these." William brought his hands from behind his back and handed her a bouquet of purple irises wrapped in silver paper.

I guess only Elizabeth gets roses, Celine thought. "Thank you," she said, as William motioned for a waiter to bring them a vase.

William sat across from her. He wore a dark, exquisitely cut Italian suit and a blue silk tie the color of his eyes.

Like a polar sea, Celine thought. At least William's incarceration hadn't hurt his looks.

The waiter arrived to take their order. "The seafood here is the best in California," William said, critically examining the wine list. "A bottle of your best wine," he told the waiter.

"I'll have a club soda," Celine said. Even though she was sure William was genuinely attracted to her—what man wouldn't be when she was wearing this dress?—she knew he wanted her help with Elizabeth. She planned to keep a clear head until she knew exactly what that involved.

"You don't want any wine?" William asked. His tone of voice held a challenge.

"Maybe later." Celine buried her face in the menu.

The waiter brought a shrimp-scampi appetizer. "Let's enjoy," William said. "I haven't had a perfect evening like this since before that parasite Tom Watts insisted on exposing my private affairs."

"Please," Celine said. "I'm trying to eat." She couldn't understand why William insisted on dwelling in the past.

"You didn't let me finish, Celine. I was going to say how refreshing it is to be with a beautiful, *mature* woman."

"I'm glad you're back," Celine purred. She hoped William had interesting plans for after dinner.

William began to talk about rich, influential people they both knew in New York and New Orleans through their families. Celine relaxed and enjoyed her truly superb dinner of baked salmon, garnished with lemons and served with a white wine sauce. William always could charm the pants off anybody when he tried. And she was flattered he was trying this hard.

She glanced up from her dessert of melt-in-your-mouth cherry cheesecake to tell him a funny, spiteful story about one of her ex-girlfriends in New Orleans. William's eyes were fixed on a blonde across the room. From the back she had a strong resemblance to Elizabeth Wakefield.

"Let's get our minds off business for tonight," she said, really annoyed. Not that William looked as if he were thinking about business.

"I didn't want to talk about Elizabeth." William sighed and looked out the window. "But since you mention her . . ."

"What have you been doing to her?" Celine asked, more sharply than she intended.

"Nothing." William laughed. "That's the whole point. I'm not going to lay a finger on her. But I am going to drive her crazy. That's fair, don't you think? She got me certified, I'll get her certified."

"Maybe," Celine said slowly. She knew Elizabeth pretty well. Elizabeth was tough. It would take a lot to turn her into a raving lunatic.

"Come," William said, rising and taking her hand. "I don't want to talk about my plans right now either. Let's go down by the ocean."

Celine sighed contentedly. She could almost feel the spray misting over her face, the taste of salt on his lips . . . "I'd like to," she said softly. "At last we'll be totally alone." Her eyes were full of meaning.

William nodded. His eyes met hers. Cool as glass. But his body, now pressing against hers, told another story.

I worry too much, she thought as she followed William out the door. *Some games with Elizabeth will be fun. And William and I are going to make quite a couple—finally.*

"You have to go in there?" Isabella stopped dead on the grass in front of the security office and stared at Jessica. "Why?"

"I don't know. They just called and said stop by right away." Jessica squinted into the morning sunlight. "Mr. Simmons probably wants to give me another lecture on morality."

"I hope that's all." Isabella looked worried.

"I can't believe Martin would really press

charges and send a student to jail." Jessica's voice wobbled a little. "If he does, he's a real creep."

"Well, good luck." Isabella shook her head and glanced across the quad. "Oops, here comes Alison, and I'm not supposed to be talking to you. Let me know what happens, Jess."

Alison passed Jessica without a word.

"What did that look mean?" Jessica murmured. Alison had been trying to hide it, but she was smiling. A nasty, triumphant smile. *The more trouble I'm in, the happier she is,* Jessica noted.

Well, Jessica Wakefield wasn't about to let haughty Alison Quinn see that she was afraid. Jessica skipped up the steps of the security office, whistling loud enough so that Alison was sure to hear.

Mr. Simmons looked up from his desk. "Ms. Wakefield? Please take a seat."

Jessica sat slowly on a metal folding chair. She had a flashback of being sent to the principal's office in grade school for laughing or passing notes in class. If only staying inside during recess was the worst form of punishment that she faced.

"I'm afraid I have bad news." Mr. Simmons cleared his throat. "Professor Martin is charging you with breaking and entering. That's a felony. Please report back to the security office tomorrow at eleven A.M. I suggest you get a lawyer right away—the right attorney could keep you out of prison."

Jessica thought she must have heard wrong. "Prison?"

Mr. Simmons gave her a small nod. *This can't be happening*, Jessica thought, panicking. *If I don't find a way to get out of this, I'll end up graduating with a degree in license-plate making.*

Elizabeth leaned against the outside brick wall of the humanities building. Now that she was convinced Professor Martin wouldn't change his mind about pressing charges, she needed a new strategy.

"I need to examine Jessica's story in the same way that I investigate pieces for the TV station," she murmured. "What exactly do I know about this case?"

Elizabeth ran the events of the past few days through her mind as if it were a microscope. Certain details of Jessica's case stood out so discretely that Elizabeth felt they must be particularly important. There was Alison Quinn's vehement dislike of both the twins, and the fact that she was the one who had told Jessica to commit the crime. Elizabeth also felt that the Thetas' prompt arrival at the campus security office was somehow significant. . . .

The answer to the puzzle seemed just out of Elizabeth's grasp. She rubbed her forehead in concentration and willed the pieces to fit together. Her thoughts returned to the most mysterious element of Jessica's foiled burglary—how had security known to set up an ambush at Professor Martin's office?

In a flash Elizabeth saw the truth. "The Thetas set Jessica up," she said out loud.

"Are you talking to the ivy on the wall?" Professor Martin's voice came from behind her.

Elizabeth whirled.

"Don't even ask," he said, leaning against the wall beside her.

"Ask what?"

"For me to drop the charges against your sister." Professor Martin raised his eyebrows and stared intensely into Elizabeth's eyes.

Elizabeth sagged against the wall. "When did you find out Jessica is my sister?"

"When I was down at the security office this morning." Professor Martin sighed and stuck his hands into his pockets. "I'm genuinely sorry, Elizabeth, but I can't let Jessica off the hook."

"I wasn't going to ask you to drop the charges." Elizabeth tried to blink back her tears.

"I guess that doesn't surprise me. Begging for leniency wouldn't really be your style." Professor Martin smiled. "Why don't you come into my office for a minute?"

Elizabeth mutely followed him into the building and down the hall to his office.

"I'll get you a can of juice out of the machine," he said. "Have a seat on the couch."

"Thanks."

Elizabeth sat on the couch and put a hand to her aching head. *He's going to put Jessica through a terrible experience, maybe even put her in jail, but I can't be mad at him. That doesn't make sense—I'm on her side and his.*

Professor Martin returned with a can of cold apple juice. She accepted it gratefully as he sat down beside her on the couch. Then he sighed and looked into her eyes.

She'd never seen him this close up. *He really is handsome,* Elizabeth thought. *But his eyes are cold—if I didn't know better, I'd think he was getting a perverse thrill out of Jessica's miserable situation.*

Professor Martin leaned a little nearer.

Is he going to kiss me? Elizabeth wondered with alarm. She jerked back, almost spilling her juice.

Professor Martin turned away.

"I'm still upset about the theft," he said. "I keep thinking that if someone hadn't tipped off security, I'd have lost my wonderful book."

"Who tipped them off?" Elizabeth tried not to sound too eager. She set her juice on the floor.

"It was an anonymous caller."

"Oh." She couldn't hide her disappointment.

"As I said, I'm truly sorry about all this, Elizabeth." He touched her hand.

He's just being friendly, Elizabeth told herself.

To her horror his fingers slid slowly up her arm.

* * *

At the door to Dickenson Hall, James gave Jessica a lingering kiss. He'd rescued her from the steps of the security office and walked her across campus. Jessica's spirits rose just a bit at the sweet, tender look in his dark-green eyes. His hands were strong as he took her face between them.

"Things can't be that bad," he said gently, wiping away her tears with his handkerchief.

"Are you going to come see me in jail?" Jessica sniffled.

"No, I'm not, because you're not going to jail."

Jessica marveled at the confident tone in his voice.

"Nobody thinks you should go to jail," James went on.

"Nobody thinks I should be a Theta, either," Jessica said, sighing. "I don't know what to do, James. All of this was supposed to get me into the Thetas. But I don't think I have a chance anymore. They won't want to pledge anybody who's socially unacceptable. Now that I've been charged with the crime, everybody's going to know about it."

James looked surprised. "The whole campus has heard already."

Jessica stood up straighter. "That's not possible. No one is supposed to know about the dare. The Thetas are protecting my good name as long as possible."

James shook his head. "Two people told me about it right away."

"Except for Isabella and Denise, the Thetas aren't supporting me at all," Jessica said slowly.

James wrapped an arm around her shoulders. "But I am," he said.

Jessica leaned into the embrace. It felt so good, she almost believed that the last days had been a bad dream.

"What are you going to do now?" James asked sympathetically.

"I guess the only thing left to do is talk to the lawyers Elizabeth has been calling," Jessica said drearily. "Liz has been telling me from the beginning that only lawyers can get me out of this."

"It's going to work out," James said firmly. "I'm here for you."

At least he isn't scared away yet, Jessica thought, trudging upstairs. *That will happen soon enough—when he sees me in one of those black-and-white-striped convict outfits.*

" 'Even though we're headed down the mountain, Lila, and obviously going the right way home, let's try using this compass and turn around,' " Lila imitated Bruce. She skipped over a tree root. " 'Why? Because my name is Bruce Patman, and I'm stupid, and that's how I like to do things.' "

Water droplets spattered her face. Lila looked

up in alarm, but it was only melting snow from a tree. "I do *not* need a storm," she murmured. "We've—*I've*—been lucky it hasn't rained or snowed so far, but eventually that has to change."

Lila walked faster. Too bad Bruce wasn't ahead of her, breaking branches and beating out a path. "Forget it," she told herself. "He might have been a little help when he was around, but look at what else you had to put up with. You'd probably be home by now if you hadn't followed him."

A white-headed woodpecker drilled slowly in a nearby tree.

"You really didn't learn, did you?" Lila asked the bird. "You got buried by an avalanche the first time you followed Bruce. So what did you do? You went right after him again. He had a compass, right? And compasses can't make mistakes—just the idiots using them."

So far, she hadn't been able to make herself stray far from what was left of the plane. Without Bruce, the mountain seemed even more terrifying and dangerous. At least near the Cessna, she had some kind of shelter. She hated to think of the animals that lurked in the shadows.

In the daytime they were nice: bunnies hopping along the trails; woodpeckers, jays, and chickadees fluttering from branch to branch. But at night . . . Lila shuddered.

Wolves. The howls weren't from the distant peaks anymore. Last night they'd been much closer. For a while the wolves had sounded as if they were right outside her campfire.

Were wolves awake in the daytime, too? Lila didn't think so. She forced herself to look back when she heard a branch break. The late-morning sun was almost directly overhead. Nothing seemed to be behind her.

"It's not much use learning about psychology, like I did last semester," she muttered, pushing down a sprig of brambles with her boot. "I should have studied carnivores. Especially their eating habits."

Her own food wouldn't be a problem for a while. She still had trail mix and a little bit of steak. Maybe food wasn't a problem for the wolves, either. They should have plenty to eat with all those rabbits around.

Probably the howls at night had been discussions of rabbits, Lila told herself, sitting down and leaning against a rock. She was exhausted. Even after the wolves had gone away, she hadn't slept well last night. Not, she told herself, because Bruce hadn't been there.

"If I rest a little, I'll be fresh for a long hike," she said aloud. "I'll actually head downhill this time, too."

As she drifted from a light doze to deep sleep, Lila's dream began. She was wrapped tight in Bruce's arms. They were in the snowy field away from the plane, right after they'd crashed. Bruce's eyes were soft and wet. . . . He was crying over her dead body.

Abruptly, the dream shifted. Again she was looking into Bruce's eyes, but now they were laughing as she tugged him out of the clear pool in the meadow. His face came closer, and closer . . . She was looking into the snarling face of a wolf. Lila awoke with a cry.

Nothing. Just trees bending over her and the dry rustle of dead pine needles.

Her knapsack was open. "I didn't leave it open," Lila said to herself, digging through it. "What . . ."

Her piece of steak was gone. Lila looked up, bewildered. Then she clapped her hand over her mouth to stifle a scream.

The tracks of a wolf led off through the soft snow.

"Byron's earlier poetry is much more optimistic than his later work. . . ."

Elizabeth knew she was babbling. Anything to distract him. Professor Martin's hand was still gently stroking her arm. He was gazing at her, a little smile tugging the corners of his mouth.

Finally Professor Martin took away his hand. Just as Elizabeth was about to let out a sigh of relief, he moved his arm to the back of the couch. His fingertips barely grazed the nape of her neck.

Elizabeth's mouth went dry. She stood up, her

knees shaking. "I, uh, I have to go," she stammered.

Professor Martin frowned. "You just got here. Why don't you finish your juice first?"

Elizabeth grabbed her juice can from the floor and drank. She stayed standing. *There is no way he's getting me back on that couch,* she thought desperately.

Professor Martin got up and walked to the door. He leaned against the doorjamb, watching her.

Elizabeth choked on the juice. She frantically stuffed the half-empty can into the trash.

Turning, Elizabeth saw that Professor Martin was blocking the door. Her blood pounded, and she could feel her face burning. Elizabeth felt like a bird in a cage, waiting for a hungry cat to pounce.

"Stop by again soon, Elizabeth." His eyes held hers. "Day or night. If you want to study or . . . need me for anything."

I can't believe I thought he was attractive. Anger was replacing some of the fear. She marched over to the door. "I have to go. I'm meeting my boyfriend."

Professor Martin didn't seem to be listening. His hand brushed her cheek; then he turned her face to his.

"Excuse me," Elizabeth gasped. "My appointment . . ."

In the space of a second his hands were everywhere: in front of the door, on her face, reaching for her shoulder. Elizabeth forced her way into the hall and ran.

Jerk! she shouted to herself as she raced down the stairs.

If he thinks he's going to get away with this, he's very, very wrong.

Chapter Ten

Winston walked down the hall to Denise's room and knocked. Denise had told him the surprise she'd promised was ready.

Winston knocked on her door again. Nobody answered, but he thought he heard giggling inside. He opened the door and peered around the dark room. "What's going on?" he wondered aloud.

Suddenly the room exploded into light.

"Surprise!" screamed a million beautiful women.

Winston's mouth dropped open. Women were everywhere: jumping out from behind chairs, bouncing on Denise's bed, looking around the door at him. Dozens of pink, green, and yellow helium balloons drifted lazily across the ceiling. A banner saying in purple letters WE LOVE YOU, WINSTON, stretched from the mirror to the window. All the women were beaming at him, only him.

I'm in heaven, Winston realized. *I must have*

died from my injuries and gone straight to heaven.

Denise pushed her way through the throng.

"Great party," Winston managed to say.

"You deserve it after all you've been through." Denise put her lips to his forehead. "Now, sit, and let me bring you a piece of cake."

He had been through a lot, Winston said to himself. He leaned back in the chair and accepted the string of a balloon from a very pretty girl he had never seen before. An attractive brunette positioned a party hat on his head.

Across the room Maia was holding up an enormous white-frosted layer cake. GET WELL, WINNIE! it said in green icing.

Denise pushed her way back through the crowd.

"Wow, that's some break." The balloon girl still stood beside Winston, pointing at his arm. She looked impressed. "So what were you doing?"

"Just Rollerblading," Winston said, casually waving his good hand in the air. "But you know how it is. I take a lot of chances when I do sports. Guess this time I just went over the edge."

"What other sports do you do?" asked a voluptuous redhead. She put her hand on the back of his chair.

"Bowling," Winston told her. "I've thought about trying parachute jumping, just for the thrill."

Denise stood there with Winston's cake and punch. He hadn't seen her come up. She looked furious. "Winston, may I speak to you privately for a minute?" she asked.

"Sure," he said. "Would you hold this?" he asked the redhead, handing off his balloon. Why was Denise upset?

"All right, Winston," Denise said when she had gotten him out in the hall. "You were getting awfully cozy with that redhead."

"I was just talking," Winston defended himself. "Why are you yelling at me? You invited her."

"No, I *didn't,*" Denise snapped. "I guess a lot of those people just heard about the party and invited themselves."

"I've never seen so many women in my life," Winston said wonderingly.

"You're going to see one less if you don't watch it," Denise warned.

"I'm sorry," Winston said. "I love the party." That was the understatement of the century.

Denise stared at him for a second. Then she turned on her heel and went back into her room. Winston followed her, trying not to smile. Maybe he wasn't being very nice, but it felt good to see Denise jealous. He had certainly eaten his heart out enough times feeling jealous about her.

"The shoe is on the other foot," he said as the female guests shouted a welcome back to him. Winston flopped into a chair again.

"What's the matter?" Candy asked with concern, kneeling beside him.

"Oh, I get a little woozy sometimes," Winston said. "You know, from the pain."

"Poor Win. Do you want me to kiss your cast and make your arm feel better?" she asked.

"I suppose it's worth a try." Winston closed his eyes and held it out.

Candy picked up his fingers that were sticking out of the cast. Winston heard a loud kissing noise. Then, to his surprise, he felt a soft kiss on his cheek.

Smiling, Winston opened his eyes. Denise was glaring straight into his face.

"That's it, Winston," she said. "I'm out of here."

"You're being ridiculous. I don't care about—" Winston began. "Enjoy the party," Denise snapped. Winston saw hurt and tears in her eyes. She marched out the door.

"It's about time you showed up," Elizabeth said irritably.

"What's your problem? I had to talk to James." Jessica tossed her book bag onto the dresser.

Elizabeth rubbed her cheeks. But no matter how hard she rubbed, she still felt Professor Martin's hand on her face.

She began to circle the room.

"The lawyer just called. He wants you to call him back right away," she said.

"Why should we even bother? Security is going

to book me tomorrow at eleven. I'm going to jail." Jessica lay back on her bed. "I won't get out until I'm a little white-haired old lady."

"I'm glad I went to all this trouble so that you can lie there and be a vegetable," Elizabeth snapped.

"What *is* the matter with you?" Jessica demanded, propping herself up on an elbow. "You'd think you were going off to solitary confinement instead of me."

"Oh, nothing." Elizabeth couldn't meet her sister's eyes. "It's just something embarrassing happened with Professor Martin."

"What? Did you try to talk to him again?"

Elizabeth slumped onto her bed. "I guess you could say that. But we didn't end up talking. He tried to . . . kiss me. It was really scary. I wasn't even sure if he was going to let me out of the office."

"I don't believe it! What are you going to do? Are you going to tell Tom?" Jessica stared at her in shock.

"No, I am *not* going to tell Tom. He'd just rush over to the humanities building and start a fight. I want to report Professor Martin to the school administration. But obviously I can't do that now." Elizabeth looked away.

"Why not?"

"That's not going to help you, is it, if he's furious with me?"

Jessica groaned. "Liz, you're making me feel horrible. That sleaze is going to think he got away with practically molesting you."

"It won't make any difference if I wait," Elizabeth assured her twin. "I jotted down some notes about the whole thing, with dates and times. I'll get him later."

"I'm really sorry, Liz," Jessica said sincerely. "You must be upset."

Elizabeth got up and started pacing again. "My relationship with him was supposed to be about poetry, and discovering truth, and . . . spiritual things. Instead he was just using all that to lure me into sitting on his lap."

"Total scum," Jessica said emphatically.

"Let's talk about you," Elizabeth said with an effort. "I know you won't like this, but we really should tell Mom and Dad what's going on. You're in serious trouble—"

"Liz, I've been in so much trouble since I started college—if I get in any more, they're going to yank me out of school," Jessica said, sounding panicked. "They'll make me live with them until I'm a hundred. Don't tell them yet. Not until we absolutely have to."

Elizabeth sighed. "OK, Jess. It's your life," she said. "But at some point Mom and Dad are going to have to be involved to pay your lawyer bills."

Jessica groaned again and stuck her head under the pillow.

"The lawyer I just got off the phone with," Elizabeth said, coming closer to Jessica's bed so that her sister would be sure to hear her through the pillow, "warned us to take this whole thing very seriously. He doesn't think you'll do jail time since this is a first offense, but he says you never know. The district attorney might decide to make an example of you."

"I still can't believe a dumb dare could go this far," Jessica mumbled.

Elizabeth yanked off the pillow. "Jessica, it wasn't a dare. The whole thing was a big, elaborate setup!" she cried. "Haven't you figured that out? You always put your head in the sand about the Thetas. They knew you would get caught. Think. Why would they do this? Does somebody hate you over there? Or are they all in on it together? I wouldn't put it past them." Elizabeth ended her tirade and waited for her sister's response.

"Well, Alison Quinn can't stand me. Some of her friends can't either, I guess," Jessica said, staring at the ceiling. "Who cares at this point? I'm going to jail."

"You'd better care," Elizabeth said fiercely. "You can't lie there and give up."

"Liz, I'm not going to go after the Thetas. I don't want to, and I don't think it would work." Jessica turned on her side and faced the wall.

Elizabeth stared at her for a second. *Oh, yes, it*

will, she thought. *Those girls are going to get what's coming to them.*

"Now, where did Liz rush off to?" Jessica said to the wall. She might be talking to a lot of walls soon—in prison. She imagined herself in solitary confinement, with only a toilet bowl for company. Jessica put the pillow over her head again and closed her eyes.

Suppose this were a prison. Blank cinder-block walls. Serial numbers and serial killers. Uniforms. Water dripping. Rats and cockroaches.

Jessica shuddered. "That just can't happen," she said.

She sat up and shook her head hard. All right. She'd just have to find a way out of this mess herself. The Thetas had dumped her. Elizabeth hadn't been able to budge Professor Martin.

"Why wouldn't that jerk listen to Liz?" Jessica asked herself.

Jessica sat up straight. Professor Martin did listen to Elizabeth—just not about the theft.

She jumped up and rummaged through Elizabeth's closet. "What would Elizabeth wear to go see him?" she muttered. "Of course, it probably doesn't matter. It's not her clothes he's interested in."

Jessica found what she thought was a trademark Elizabeth outfit: new, pressed blue jeans, sandals, and a T-shirt that said THE EARTH IS YOUR

MOTHER. She quickly changed and located the small tape recorder that Elizabeth used in her reporting work. Jessica checked the batteries and put it in her backpack.

Then she looked in the mirror. Her face would be important.

Silky blond hair, a dimple in the left cheek of her smile, blue-green eyes the color of a summer sea. She looked great.

"I think it's time to talk to that sleazebag professor again, Elizabeth," she told her reflection.

"Damn!" Bruce gasped, clutching his injured wrist. He slammed his good hand into the tree that had just slashed him with a branch.

Then he crushed the lousy compass under his heel and slid down a steep, snow-covered slope. He gritted his teeth, remembering what a fool he'd felt like while Lila screamed at him yesterday.

He wiped sweat from his forehead and paused to rest by a pool at the foot of a tree. His reflection wavered in the clear water.

Bruce leaned forward and looked at himself. He hadn't shaved in four days. Black stubble covered his lower face like a bandit. His thick brown hair stuck up in the back.

Bruce grinned. "I'm not a pampered city boy anymore," he told his reflection.

He glanced at the sky. The sun was touching the tops of the trees. Time to make camp. He saw a clearing just ahead, ringed by thick bushes. Bruce dumped his knapsack on the ground and took out his last steak sandwich.

His food was about gone—he wished he knew how to hunt.

"What lives out here anyway?" Bruce muttered. "All I've seen are birds and a weasel."

He picked up a large dead branch from the ground and held it up to use as a club.

The pine needles rattled like skeletons. The forest was darkening into vague shapes and shadows as the sun set. Bruce wondered if Lila was afraid at night—if she was afraid now, as she watched night fall. "Did I act like a world-class jerk, leaving her?" he murmured. "Not really. She was worse." But what if Lila was already dead because he wasn't around? Lying facedown and bloody, already starting to rot?

Bruce shuddered. He should put Lila out of his mind. His own survival was what he had to concentrate on now.

He saw a small white rabbit just ahead, on the edge of a group of trees. "OK, bunny," Bruce said softly. "Just hold still, while I get a little closer. . . ."

The rabbit watched him, twitching its pink nose.

Bruce lofted his stick.

The rabbit's ears pointed forward. It whirled and ran soundlessly into the forest. Bruce could see it for only a second before it vanished into the gloom.

"Damn!" he cried. "I almost had you."

Black night had fallen. He could barely see where he was going. Nights in the woods were different from the city nights he was used to; the darkness was complete until the moon rose. Soon he wouldn't be able to see his hand before his face.

Bruce trudged along, hardly caring if he ran into trees. He couldn't believe how crushed he was over not being able to kill a measly rabbit.

"I screwed up," he said out loud. With no one to hear him, he could say whatever he wanted.

Maybe I screwed up a lot of other things, too, Bruce thought, scuffing his feet through the dead, fragrant pine needles. Maybe the Sigma brothers thought he was great, but a lot of them were screwups too.

Bruce shook his head to try to clear it of thoughts. That was the trouble with being out here: there was nothing to do but think. Looking around, Bruce realized that he'd been walking aimlessly, making no effort to keep track of his direction.

Where was his campsite? His food, his blanket . . . He began to run through the forest. Branches whipped his face and creaked menacingly behind him. The snow was refreezing.

Bruce slipped and fell. The forest was completely silent, except for the sound of wind whistling through the trees.

"Lila!" he yelled. *"Somebody!"*

* * *

"Don't run away again," Winston begged. "Denise, please. You haven't talked to me since the party. I can't stand much more of this!"

Denise kept walking along the path to her evening sociology class.

"I admit I'm a jerk, and inconsiderate, and brag too much," Winston said quickly.

Denise stopped and turned around. "I already knew all that."

"I'll even admit I'm terrible at sports." Winston was rewarded by Denise's tiny smile.

Progress. Winston walked slowly toward her, as if she were a wild deer who might bolt. Yesterday when he'd set his dinner tray next to hers, she'd moved to a new seat. Same thing at breakfast. He didn't know where she'd had lunch.

"Win, I don't know what we're going to do . . ." Denise began.

To Winston's dismay he saw Candy coming up the path straight toward him. She was tossing her book bag in the air and humming. *Let her not speak to me,* Winston prayed. *Let her be late for class. Very, very late for class and rush right on by.*

"Hey, Win!" Candy was closing in on him.

Winston's mind was racing. If he answered her, he would be in more trouble with Denise. If he kept his mouth shut, he'd look like a jerk. *I never thought I'd be* sorry *that a pretty girl—or any girl for that matter—wanted to talk to me.*

"Win?" Candy stood next to his elbow. "Did my treatment help your arm?" She gently patted his cast and grinned at Denise.

"Yeah," Winston said. He didn't dare look at Denise. He could feel the strength of her glare through the back of his head. "It's much better."

"Stop by later for a follow-up treatment if you want. You can't be too careful." Candy laughed and continued up the path.

Winston heard Denise take a sharp breath.

"Denise, Candy didn't mean anything," Winston began desperately. "She certainly didn't mean what you think she did."

"Go away, Winston." Denise had tears in her eyes. She hugged her books to her chest. "Please. Just go away."

Chapter Eleven

"What are your plans after law school, Steven?" Mr. Winkler asked.

Steven tied the strings of an apron around Mr. Winkler's waist. It had a picture of a red chili pepper on it saying I'M HOT TO COOK!

"I suppose I'll go into international law," he replied.

"How does chicken Kiev sound for dinner? I've already started it in the oven," Billie said to her mother, giving Steven an encouraging smile. Billie looked a lot like her mom. Same blue eyes, dark hair, small, compact frame. Although Billie's mother had a few streaks of gray in her hair, she was still pretty. *She's not really old. Would it be such a shock to her that Billie and I are living together?* Steven wondered.

"Chicken sounds delicious, dear. Isn't this nice, all of us making dinner together?" Mrs. Winkler looked into the freezer.

"International law is definitely a growing field," Billie's father said.

Billie's smile at Steven grew more intense.

"I hope it will be a good career," Steven said carefully. *Sound respectable,* he told himself.

Steven went over to the cabinet where they kept the spices and got out tarragon to chop for the chicken. Even if conversation with his girlfriend's parents was a strain, he was glad to see Billie again.

He hadn't even spoken to her in two days. She must have been sight-seeing with her parents till she dropped, because every time he called, she was out. Finally she had come by Mike's to give him a quick hug and invite him to dinner that night.

"I'll take that tarragon," Billie said, leaning over and kissing him. Both her parents watched.

"What do you want us to do, Billie?" her mother asked, smiling a little.

"Well—you can set the table, Daddy. And, Mom, I was going to make up a cheesecake. I already bought the shell, so we just have to mix the filling. . . ."

"Where are the pans?" Steven asked, sounding fake even to himself. He saw Mr. Winkler watching him intently, his hand full of forks.

"In the open drawer right in front of you," Mr. Winkler said, reaching around him to hand him a pan. "Are your eyes all right?"

"Yes," Steven said. He tried to motion Billie with his head to meet him in the bedroom.

Mr. Winkler took back the pan and filled it with water. He set it on a burner and tried to light the stove.

Without thinking Steven expertly jiggled the stove so that the flame from the pilot light could reach the burner.

"Amazing you knew how to do that," said Mr. Winkler, shuffling his handful of forks.

"Steven's . . . uh . . . teaching me to cook Japanese food," Billie said hastily. "That's why he knows how to work the stove."

"Oh, I see," said Mrs. Winkler, flipping the chicken in the baking pan. "It's nice that men these days can cook. Most of the young men in my day just sat down at the table and waited to be fed."

Steven ducked out of the kitchen before anyone could ask him exactly how to cook Japanese. He glanced in the bedroom. Light-green curtains and matching spread. Girl things, like a pink hairbrush and a romance novel, were neatly lined up on the bureau. Immaculate. He realized with a pang that he'd been swept out of Billie's existence, even if it was just temporary.

"Steven!" Billie called. "We're about ready to eat."

Steven sighed. Billie had missed his message about meeting in the bedroom. He had to get her alone to explain to her the weird thing that was going on with the bedroom ceiling at night.

Steven helped Billie carry food to the table she'd set up in the living room and tried to think of a good conversation opener. Preferably one that wouldn't tell Billie's parents something they shouldn't know.

Safer to talk about the past, maybe. "So what was it like in the sixties, when you got married?" he asked.

"We got married during college," Mrs. Winkler said. "Back then that was normal. Unfortunately, a lot of our friends who were married around the same time are divorced now."

"Well, I guess that's why Billie—I mean people—I mean anyone should live together before they get married," Steven finished in a desperate rush. "I mean—"

Billie kicked him so hard under the table, the dishes rattled.

"Would you excuse me?" Steven finished lamely, getting up and hurrying into the bathroom. A moment later Billie followed.

"I'm sorry," he said before she could get out a word.

"It's OK. You're trying." Billie sighed deeply.

"Yeah." Steven kissed her forehead.

"I just have to tell them about us soon." Billie leaned against the tile wall. "But I have to think of a way not to shock them out of their socks."

"I need to tell you something," Steven began. "I was really missing you the first night your parents were here. . . ."

Steven heard a dish clatter in the living room. He and Billie glanced nervously at the door.

"So I banged on Mike's ceiling with a broom to say good night," Steven went on quickly. "And your parents banged back and said good night. I don't know if they recognized my voice."

"My parents were sleeping in the bedroom! I was on the couch." Billie looked appalled.

"Well, of course I didn't do it again," Steven said quickly. "But they did."

"What?" Billie stared at him.

"Last night they pounded on the floor and yelled 'Good night.'"

Billie looked as though she might lose her mind. "Let's just hope they *didn't* recognize your voice. One more slip, and they're going to know for sure we live together."

"Let's get them talking about when you were a little girl," Steven suggested. "Parents always love that."

"Oh, goody," Billie said, rolling her eyes. "Maybe my mother has some embarrassing pictures in her wallet of me with braces. Wait, I'll leave first. You stay in here for a while so they won't know we're conspiring."

Steven heard Billie's chair scrape as she sat back down.

"So tell me, since I'm kind of behind the times. Do young people use the bathroom together these days?" he heard Mr. Winkler ask.

Steven groaned. This wasn't going well at all.

William stepped into the medicine closet with Andrea, the student intern, and closed the door. He pulled her to him roughly and kissed her with carefully executed passion.

The medicine closet smelled of tranquilizers, bandages, and disinfectant. He wished she didn't make him do this. Unfortunately, it was necessary, or she wouldn't let him out of the institution.

"When will you be back?" she whispered.

"Early tomorrow afternoon," he whispered back. "I'll just slip into the arts-and-crafts room and work on my painting. Now, let me get out of here. I've got an appointment."

He did. It was an important one: stalking Elizabeth Wakefield.

"OK," Andrea said softly. She opened the closet door and looked down the hallway. Then she motioned him out.

William followed her down the hall at a respectful patient-to-therapist distance. A couple of the other male inmates in the dangerous ward were lying on the floor.

"Don't you guys want to get up and watch TV or something?" Andrea asked the men gently. They didn't respond.

"They're knocked out from tranquilizers," William said, looking contemptuously at them. He never took his medication. The institution doctors liked to drug the patients into premature senility just to make them easier to manage.

Andrea sighed and unlocked the door to the ward. William turned his cold stare on Andrea's slightly pudgy body.

She looked back at him. William's face lit up with a wistful smile. He eased around her out the door, taking care to maximize body contact. Then he waved good-bye and tiptoed down the dimly lit corridor.

This was the dangerous part. Patients from the locked ward weren't supposed to be wandering the halls by themselves. If he got caught, he'd either have to claim he was delusional or run for his final escape.

His footsteps tapped hollowly down the corridor. Occasionally he heard a distant hoot or scream from a disturbed patient. "I don't want to leave for good now," he whispered as he passed the silent, blank doors of the psychiatrists' offices. "I'm very safe here. I can't be accused of anything. Not even if Sweet Valley University turns into a madhouse. . . ."

Like this place. He didn't want to stay there too long. How would he know if he started to go crazy?

Sometimes he worried that just being there

would make his brain infected. *These trips out to the world are keeping me sane*, he thought. Elizabeth was keeping him sane. "Elizabeth," he said softly as he punched the combination to the outside door.

He hurried to his car, slipping on a lab coat as he went. "Now I'm a highly esteemed doctor," William muttered, starting the ignition. "All it takes is a cheap white jacket. Why do those idiots have any say over my life? Just because of what happened with Elizabeth."

He'd only tried to hurt her that once. And it hadn't really been his fault—she'd provoked him into losing his temper. William figured that Elizabeth was too smart a girl to make that happen again.

Tonight he was going to try something a little different. "I'm tired of staring at Elizabeth's window!" he shouted over the powerful growl of the engine. For a while that had been enough, but it wasn't anymore. Tonight he would be with her everywhere, unseen.

I love her, William thought. *What could possibly be crazy about that?*

Steven opened the medicine cabinet to get a couple of aspirin before he went back out to the living room. *I haven't had a headache like this since we tried to hide Jessica's marriage from my parents*, he thought.

As Steven reached for the bottle, he saw the one thing Billie had forgotten to hide. His after-shave was sitting next to the sink. Steven grabbed it and looked quickly around. Where could he put it? Her nosy parents might look anywhere.

Frantically Steven tucked the aftershave into his belt and pulled his shirt over it.

"Steven, Billie's telling us about the first time you two went out together. Do you want to add to her story?" Mrs. Winkler greeted him when he stepped outside the bathroom.

"No—I mean, yes," Steven grunted. He was trying to puff out his stomach. The aftershave was slipping out of his belt, and he was only halfway across the living room.

The aftershave dropped down his leg and out of his pants and rolled across the floor toward Billie's parents. Steven could feel his face turning purple.

"Is that how you usually carry your after-shave?" asked Mrs. Winkler, laughing.

"No," Steven mumbled.

"What a coincidence—you and Don use the same brand," Mrs. Winkler went on.

"That's *my* aftershave!" Mr. Winkler roared. "What in the world are you two *doing*?"

She would know that voice anywhere. Deep, sexy, and right next to her ear. "Hey, Nina," Bryan was saying.

Nina felt relief flood through her. She stopped short just before the door to her dorm. So he was still speaking to her. "Hi, Bryan."

"How have you been?" Bryan asked. His tone was careless, not intense the way it usually was.

"I've been OK," she said. That was almost true. Two days after their breakup, she could almost convince herself that she was getting used to being without him—at least she could concentrate on something besides him for five minutes now. The first day she had thought about him constantly.

"I've been OK too," Bryan said stiffly.

He's mad because I didn't go to that BSU meeting yesterday, Nina thought. *So what else is new?*

She took a step toward her dorm and hesitated. "You could come up," she said. "You know, just for a minute." Nina had to admit that she did feel guilty about ditching the meeting without telling him.

"Maybe I shouldn't." Bryan faced her. "We could go to the coffeehouse. I want to ask you something."

Nina took a step in the direction of the coffeehouse. Then she shook her head. "This is silly. If you need to ask me something, there's no reason we have to walk all the way over there. I can make us a cup of instant coffee in my room."

"OK." Bryan seemed reluctant. "But I don't want you to get the wrong idea."

"I won't," Nina said firmly. "It'll be just for a minute."

Nina was aware of Bryan's eyes as he followed her up the stairs. She wished she could stop the ridiculous hammering of her heart. *I never thought I'd get so riled up over a cup of coffee,* Nina said to herself. *I wonder if this means anything to Bryan?*

Nina unlocked the door to her room and quickly took down two mugs from the shelf above her desk. She poured a teaspoon of coffee into each of them and ducked into the hall to fill them from the hot-water dispenser.

When she came back, Bryan was sitting on the bed. Nina's throat tightened. He was definitely the best-looking man on campus. Really, on earth. "What did you want to ask me?" She handed him a mug of coffee and quickly turned away from him to stir her own.

"I want to know why you didn't come to the BSU meeting yesterday."

"Do you really have to ask? Don't you remember what happened at the last one?" Nina still didn't look at him. She perched on the edge of her desk.

"We disagreed about policy. That doesn't mean we're enemies. Even if we are broken up . . ." Bryan's voice faltered. "You can still come to the meetings."

Nina shook her head. "I don't agree with you

about who should be included in the March Against Racism."

"Nina, there's room for ideological differences in the BSU."

"Sometimes it doesn't seem like it." Nina sat beside him on the bed. *I'm just sitting here because the desk is so hard*, she told herself.

The mattress dipped under her weight, and their legs touched. Nina tried to move away, but the bed kept sinking back.

Nina looked into Bryan's face, inches from her own. Their lips touched; then he pulled away slightly. Nina's heart hammered. She leaned forward and brought her lips to his again. His mouth opened to hers, and he slowly pushed her back on the bed.

Then he sat up abruptly. "Sorry."

"Me too," Nina said quickly. "We shouldn't do that." Their legs were still touching, and chills were still chasing up and down her spine.

"I'd like you to come to the next meeting, tomorrow afternoon at one," Bryan said, rising. "We'll discuss what you brought up at the last meeting—whether to ask the general student body to march with us."

"OK," Nina said, surprised but pleased. "I'll be there."

"I should go now." Bryan moved toward the door.

"Yeah, you should go," Nina said, trying not to sound disappointed.

I will go to the next meeting, she thought, watching his confident, determined steps as he went down the hall.

"Something *is* going on here," said Billie. "Mom, Dad, sit down. There's something I have to tell you. I think you'd better be sitting when you hear it."

"I hope whatever it is doesn't stop my old heart," said Mr. Winkler, falling backward onto the couch and clutching his chest.

Steven looked at him in surprise. That sounded like a joke.

"I'd better sit too," Mrs. Winkler added, plopping onto the couch next to her husband.

Steven groaned inwardly.

The Winklers looked at Billie expectantly. Steven edged toward the front door.

"Steven, come back," Billie said. The parental heads swiveled to stare at him.

"I wasn't sure I should stay," he mumbled.

"Billie seems sure," said Mrs. Winkler, smiling a little.

Trapped, Steven leaned against the door. To his horror Billie said, "Steven, come here. Let's do this together."

Steven decided he would just let Billie's parents yell at him if they wanted to. He wouldn't say a word in his defense.

"Please don't tell me you're living together,"

Mrs. Winkler said, frowning. Her face twitched.

"I'm sorry, Mom. I don't want to disappoint you, or for you to think I don't have any morals . . ." Billie stammered.

"How do you intend to support my daughter?" Mr. Winkler demanded of Steven.

"I . . . don't know." Steven felt a sweat break out on his forehead. Why would he support Billie? She planned to be a tax attorney; she would probably make bigger bucks than he did.

Billie's parents looked at each other. "I can't stand this for another minute," said Mrs. Winkler.

"Neither can I," Mr. Winkler said solemnly.

Billie's parents looked at each other and started laughing hysterically. "This is such a riot," Mrs. Winkler gasped. "You two are the worst actors I've ever seen."

"You knew all along!" Billie cried. "You were just torturing us."

Chapter Twelve

"Everyone's talking about how wonderful you've been through all this," Isabella said, taking Jessica's arm and pulling her up the steps to Theta House. "The least we can do is give you breakfast."

"You could get in trouble," Jessica protested halfheartedly. She let Isabella lead her inside the sorority. *I deserve breakfast,* she thought. *I'm doing enough suffering for the Thetas. I'd like to know it's worth it.* She hadn't been able to find Professor Martin yesterday to try out her plan on him. Not knowing whether or not the plan would work was bringing her tension level to breaking point.

"Don't worry." Isabella shrugged. "Alison's the only person who really doesn't want you around. And she told me yesterday she wouldn't be at the brunch."

"Well, don't desert me," Jessica said, looking

nervously around the entryway. "Does everybody else know I'm coming?"

"Sure." Isabella tugged her arm.

Jessica stood at the edge of the dining room. A buffet table to the side of the room was loaded with plates of scrambled eggs and sausage. Croissants and blueberry muffins crowded a silver tray.

"Hey, Jess!" Denise hurried over, carrying her plate of food. "Help yourself to the buffet."

"Thanks—it looks good," Jessica said. Maybe she did feel like eating something after all, for the first time since her life had exploded three days ago. She picked up a plate.

"We're really glad you could make it, Jessica," said Kimberly Schyler, the Theta treasurer, walking over to stand with Denise. "A group of us asked Isabella to make sure you came."

"Thanks." Jessica smiled. She could feel herself beginning to relax just a little.

"Let's sit." Isabella looked around. "There's room at the other end of the table."

Jessica pulled back a chair, balancing her plate of food in her other hand. Suddenly a hand snaked around her and shoved the chair in against the table.

"Just what do you think *you're* doing?" Alison Quinn hissed. "How dare you show up at this house!"

Jessica stared at Alison in shock. Alison looked

angry enough to hit her. *Why*? Jessica wondered. Her stomach churned. *This isn't about protecting the sorority or my eating a Theta croissant. Alison has got some horrible personal problem with me.*

"I invited Jessica," Isabella said calmly, moving close to her. "Please sit down, Jess."

"I should just go." Jessica set her plate of food on the table.

Alison glared at Isabella. "Yes, she should. That girl is jeopardizing this entire sorority! I told her not to come here. Now, get out, Jessica, for the last time!"

"Stay, Jessica," said Denise, moving up next to Isabella.

Jessica felt like the birdie in a badminton game.

"Jessica, you don't have the class to belong to this sorority," Alison said coldly, sounding more in control. "We were obviously very wrong to let you repledge."

Jessica was determined to stand her ground. "Why were you wrong, Alison?" she asked.

"Do you really have to ask?" Alison demanded. "After what you've done?"

"You asked me to steal that book," Jessica said, her voice rising. "Now I don't have any class because of that?"

"You don't have any class, period." Alison narrowed her eyes. "Everyone at this school knows about your wild behavior last semester, ending in a disgusting marriage to a motorcycle freak. Now you've involved this sorority in the worst scandal of its history: The whole campus knows we were pledging a common thief. Leave, Jessica. You're bringing us down."

Feel free to jump in anytime, Jessica willed her friends.

Nobody said anything. Isabella shook her head and motioned slightly toward the door.

"Here's what we're going to do," William said.

Celine broke an apple Danish in two and nibbled half. She wasn't sure she was up to doing anything. It was too early in the morning by about three hours.

She would have preferred to talk about their evening together. William had certainly entertained her in style the night before last. Celine's red lips curved in a smile as she remembered his tender compliments by the ocean. They'd run along the beach in their bare feet while the cool waves curled around their toes, then shared darkness and a room. . . . She'd woken up knowing blissfully that it hadn't been a dream.

Or maybe it had. The morning light had brought back the harsh reality of William's precarious situation. He'd left her at dawn, almost without a word.

Now Celine looked around the seedy little diner at the beefy truck drivers, insurance salesmen with plastic briefcases, and harried waitresses in polyester aprons. She'd had to drive twenty miles to this coffeehouse just to eat breakfast so that William wouldn't be recognized. William seemed to have forgotten he had ever recognized *her,* at least as an attractive woman.

He held out a white rose knotted in a scarf. "Put this on Elizabeth's desk in the library. She studies in the same place every morning for three hours. As soon as she goes to get a drink or something, just drop off the rose."

Celine frowned. Roses were still for Elizabeth. Even if she got them in a warped way. Had he completely forgotten their night at the ocean?

"Why?" she asked. "What do you think she's going to do when she finds it?"

"It's all part of the plan."

"What plan?" Celine poured herself another cup of coffee. She'd better wake up, before she signed on for something she'd regret.

"I told you, Celine. We're going to play some games." William lounged back in his chair.

Celine shivered. "Sweetheart, you sound positively malicious. I'm not sure these so-called games are such a hot idea."

"Oh, come on, Celine." William sounded impatient. "It's no big deal. We're not going to hurt her, just scare her a little."

"She'll be scared, all right." Celine looked at him over the brim of her coffee cup, trying to evaluate William's mental state. He looked cool and elegant, a little bored. Completely in control. The opposite of the way he had looked when he and the other secret-society members had been trying to throw Elizabeth in a pit last semester.

"She'll know the rose is from you," Celine pointed out. "A *white* rose? You practically buried her in them last semester."

"Sometimes I'd like to bury her," William muttered. "Think, Celine. Elizabeth knows I'm locked up. Therefore, the rose can't be from me. But I did used to give her white roses. So what will it mean when she gets another one? She'll feel in danger, but she won't know from whom. Psychologically, what could be worse?"

"You've definitely got it all thought out," Celine said sourly. She didn't want William to spend so much time thinking about Elizabeth. For one thing, all of these tricks were likely to land them in major trouble at some point. The school authorities might make her a janitor instead of a food server if they caught her with William again.

But what really bothered her was that William still seemed interested in Elizabeth romantically. Why else would he spend all his free time cooking up ways to get Snow White's undivided attention?

"Let's go," William said, rising and picking up the check. "I don't want the rose to wilt."

Celine opened her mouth to tell him that she would just take her own sweet time with her breakfast.

William smiled his most charming smile. "I'd like to see you tonight, after all our business is taken care of," he said. "I'll show you a little restaurant in the mountains. It serves delicious northern-Italian food, and the atmosphere is very . . . intimate."

"All right." Celine picked up the rose. She knew she was being schmoozed, but things were balancing out. Getting a limp rose wasn't as good as an expensive dinner.

"While you're taking care of that little prank, I'll be doing something even more impressive."

"What?" Celine demanded.

"The details aren't important. Let's just say it's too special for me to entrust to someone else." William's smug smile was unnerving.

"That sounds risky."

"Don't worry your pretty Southern head over it, Celine. I've got everything under control."

"There is nowhere else on this campus Isabella could be," Elizabeth said to herself. She stood in the center of the quad, trying to spot Isabella's mane of dark hair in the rush-hour student traffic walking to morning classes.

Elizabeth was glad she had something pressing to do. It kept her mind off what had happened yesterday with Professor Martin. "I wonder if I'll get any sleep until I report him," she murmured. If last night was any indication, she wouldn't.

"If I can't find Isabella, I'll be out of ideas," she said to herself. "I'll have to call Mom and Dad, even if Jessica has a fit."

Elizabeth swallowed, trying not to feel frantic. *Think!* she commanded herself. Isabella couldn't have evaporated.

"Tom doesn't know where she is. Danny thinks she's studying for a big test somewhere, but he can't find her either," Elizabeth said aloud. "The Thetas say they don't know where she is—although I trust them about as far as I can throw them."

Elizabeth sat on a bench in front of the library and put her head in her hands. "Where does a party girl like Isabella go when she doesn't want to be found?" she asked herself.

Then she knew. "The one place I didn't look," Elizabeth muttered, running to the door of the library.

She found Isabella in the reading room. "Hey, Isabella," Elizabeth said eagerly, pulling up a chair from the next carrel.

Isabella lifted her head from the desk. Her eyes had dark rings around them, and even her clothes were rumpled.

"Did you spend the night in here?" Elizabeth asked in amazement.

"Did I? I guess so. Then I had breakfast, and when I woke up, I was here again." Isabella put her head down on her arms and yawned. "Don't ever take astronomy, Elizabeth. Not unless you want to memorize the name of every Cepheid variable in the galaxy."

"Thanks for the hint." Out of the corner of her eye, Elizabeth saw the library worker in the wheelchair roll between the stacks, pulling behind him a cart of books to be shelved. "May I ask you something?"

"Anything," Isabella said wearily.

"It's about Jessica and the sorority dare." Elizabeth tried not to sound too eager.

"What about it?" Isabella asked. "Of course, you're not supposed to know it was a sorority dare."

Elizabeth chose to ignore Isabella's comment. "Did you know Professor Martin is pressing criminal charges against Jessica?"

Isabella looked shocked. "No. Really?"

"This morning it's official." Elizabeth leaned closer. "Isabella, I need your help in getting Jessica out of this mess."

"You've got it," Isabella said slowly. "I can't believe things went this far. Jessica must be going out of her mind. So what do you want me to do?"

"Tell security that the sorority put Jessica up to the theft. And who in the sorority. Whose idea was it for Jessica to steal the Byron book?"

"Alison's," said Isabella. "The rest of the sisters would have just let Jessica repledge, and that would have been the end of it."

"Why didn't anyone stop Alison from making

Jessica do something so crazy?" Elizabeth asked irritably. Sorority sisters had a herd mentality.

"I tried to, but not hard enough, I guess." Isabella shrugged. "It didn't seem like such a big deal. I really didn't think Jessica would get caught. Stealing a book was something I thought she'd be good at."

Elizabeth winced. Isabella was right, but the description of her twin wasn't flattering.

"So why do you think Alison wanted Jessica to do the dare?" Elizabeth asked.

"I don't know. She doesn't like her much. But I thought it was pretty funny when Alison called Jessica a thief at brunch this morning. Alison is always stealing. The sorority has had to cover for her a couple of times when she got caught. It's no wonder she thought up making Jess steal the book."

"I think Alison wanted Jessica to get caught and lose her chance of becoming a Theta for good," Elizabeth said. "Somebody called security the night of the theft and set Jessica up. Was it Alison?"

"It could have been." Isabella looked thoughtful. "Very likely. But I don't know for sure."

"Would you be willing to tell security what you just told me?" Elizabeth mentally crossed her fingers. What if Isabella refused, because it would get her into trouble with the Thetas?

Isabella ran her hands through her thick black

hair. "I know I'm supposed to stick with the sorority do or die, but as far as I'm concerned, that means bailing Jessica out of the trouble we got her in."

"Thanks, Isabella," Elizabeth said gratefully.

"I'm going home to take a shower, but I'll be back here in a while. Just come get me if you need me." Isabella yawned again. "Anything's better than living in the library, right?"

For you and Jessica, I'm sure of it, Elizabeth thought. "Right," she said.

After Isabella left, Elizabeth sat tapping a pencil against the table. She collected her thoughts for a few moments, then grabbed her notebooks and jumped up. So now she'd go tell the security officers . . . what?

"I know what happened, but I can't really prove it," she mumbled, sinking back into her chair. "Alison will just say she had nothing to do with setting up Jessica, and probably that the sorority didn't either. Maybe when the dust settles, most of the Thetas will admit the sorority *was* behind the theft, but by then Jessica will have spent a couple of days in jail."

The library staffer in the wheelchair rolled by—not close, but just close enough so that the movement distracted her. Elizabeth's skin prickled.

She looked up. He was busily shelving books, seeming totally unaware that she was even sitting there.

So now I know for sure Alison was behind the plot, Elizabeth said to herself, forcing her mind back onto her problem. *And she must have made the call to security.*

The trouble was proving it.

"Got it!" she yelled, smacking the desk. The empty library faintly echoed her words. *If there was a call, campus security must have a record of it,* Elizabeth thought, leaping to her feet. She raced off to the pay phone on the landing.

When they tell me that call came from Theta House, this case will be closed, she thought.

"Denise?" Winston said tentatively, walking into the bathroom. She looked up from the sink and dried her face with a towel.

Progress, Winston thought. At least she hadn't ordered him to go away. He leaned on the sink beside hers.

"What do you want?" she asked. Winston couldn't bear the hint of suspicion in her voice.

"To apologize," he said, taking her hand. "I really am sorry. I mean, I've been jealous of you enough times to know it isn't fun. If you *are* jealous, that is. I have a hard time believing you could be. I mean, you could date any guy on campus. Why should you care if some girl kisses my cast?"

Mistake to bring that up, he thought with alarm. *Especially since it wasn't just the cast that got kissed.*

"Winston, my feelings were really *hurt.*" Denise shook her hand free. She picked up a jar of peach moisturizer and began rubbing it into her face. "Why couldn't you just figure out that of course I don't like it when you let other women fawn over you?"

"They weren't fawning," Winston said uncomfortably. "They were just trying to be nice. I *am* an invalid." He lifted his broken arm.

Denise didn't even look at it. *Well, it was worth a try,* Winston thought.

"Let's reverse the situation," she said. "Suppose I had sixty guys packed into a room and they were all feeding me chocolates and swooning over my poor hurt arm and kissing me . . ."

"The kiss," Winston said with a sigh. "I knew we were leading up to that. I guess I should have pretended to gag after Candy kissed me."

"See, that's just it." Denise pointed a loofah at him. "You would have had to *pretend* to gag. You liked kissing her."

"I didn't like it." *So why do I feel guilty?* he thought. "Or maybe I did, but not—"

Winston had to move fast to grab Denise's wrist before she left the bathroom. "You can't go out there covered with pink goo," he said. Actually, she could. It only clarified the perfect oval shape of her face.

"Watch me." Denise tried to pull free.

"Just let me finish!" Winston almost shouted.

He dropped her hand. A one-armed man was no match for her anyway.

Denise folded her arms, but she didn't go.

"I did like it that all those girls were paying attention to me, including Candy," Winston said, trying to sound calmer. He was probably on his very last chance with Denise. He had to get this to come out right. "But I only liked it because you were watching. I thought you would see that I wasn't just some klutz who crashes into a tree and breaks into pieces the first time he tries Rollerblading."

Denise looked at him thoughtfully, rubbing the moisturizer into her face. "You know, you really understand women, Win. That's one reason you're so popular with them."

"I am?" Winston was astonished. "Not even you could believe that, Denise. You know me too well. Most women go for real he-man types, like Bruce Patman. The kind of guy who eats raw bear meat."

Denise made a face. "You're caring, and understanding, and gentle, Win," she said. "You could have more women than any guy on campus."

The door to the bathroom slowly cracked open. "Is this fight going to last a long time?" Candy asked. "A few of us would like to use this bathroom for its intended purpose."

"You might want to use the one on the second floor," Denise said crisply. "We may be in here another hour."

The door banged shut. "Unless you want me to leave and her to come in," Denise added.

"Don't be silly. Of course I only want to be in the bathroom with you." Winston turned on the cold water in his sink and splashed water over his face to cool it off. He was still far from out of trouble. "I'm not interested in anybody but you. Don't you know that?"

"I wasn't sure." Denise shrugged.

"You're the love of my life," Winston said simply.

"Really?" Denise's brilliant blue eyes were soft.

"Of course." Winston didn't even have to think about that one. He watched the water fill the sink. Didn't Denise realize that his heart pounded and leaped just at the sight of her? He was obsessed with her.

"Winston, is that water still running?" Maia asked authoritatively through the closed door. "In case you haven't heard, California is in a water crisis."

Winston noticed that the water was flooding over the basin. Denise shut it off. "Sorry!" she yelled to Maia. "There's just one more thing," she said to Winston.

Winston groaned silently. Maybe he did understand women. There was always just one more thing with them.

"Kissing Candy," Denise said, shaking out her towel and folding it.

"If you really think about what happened, it was nothing," Winston argued. "You know what Candy's like. She was just joking around. And *she* kissed me. I didn't kiss her. And I don't want to."

Denise said nothing.

"Aren't you used to my doing stupid things?" Winston entreated. "Please forgive me?"

"Why don't we go discuss this in my room? You can give me a one-armed back rub and tell me all the reasons why I should let you off the hook."

"Do you have a few hours?" Winston let out an enormous sigh of relief.

Denise ran her hands behind his ears and touched her lips to his forehead. "For you I've got all day."

Chapter Thirteen

Jessica swung onto the walk leading to the humanities building. "No one had better mess with me today," she muttered. A storm front had rolled in from the Pacific since that disastrous Theta brunch, and low, fast-moving gray clouds chased her along the path. Perfect weather to go call on a jerk professor.

Jessica stopped in front of Professor Martin's office to compose herself. She checked the tape recorder in her backpack one last time. *Be Elizabeth,* she told herself.

Since she hadn't been able to find Martin the day before, she'd put on Elizabeth's clothes again for another try. It was a little much to wear an EARTH IS YOUR MOTHER T-shirt twice in two days. Martin had better make it worth her while.

It was surprising James hadn't commented on how bizarre she looked when he'd walked her over there. He must have extremely good manners.

"This isn't really dangerous," Jessica said to herself. "James will be here in an hour if I don't show up at the frat house." She felt better knowing that she had that security. She intended to tease Professor Martin, and people who were teased sometimes turned ugly.

Jessica knocked on the office door.

Professor Martin opened it. "Elizabeth," he said, looking concerned. "Are you all right? You went flying out of here yesterday."

Jessica gave him an uncertain smile. "I . . . just had to hurry off somewhere," she said. "But I didn't want you to think anything was wrong."

"Come in and talk. We haven't said a word about our project in days."

I'll just bet you want to talk about poetry, Jessica thought. He really did seem kind of nice and unassuming. That must be how he'd gotten to Elizabeth. *Don't let down your guard,* Jessica reminded herself.

Jessica slowly followed him inside and stopped in the middle of the room. Professor Martin sat at his desk. He was watching her intently. A little too intently. Her stomach flip-flopped, even though things were going exactly as she had hoped.

Jessica sauntered over to the desk and leaned against it. She ran a hand through her hair. "May I ask you something, *George*?"

Professor Martin looked curious. "Of course. You can ask me anything, Elizabeth."

Jessica sat on the desk. That look in his eyes . . . She shivered. That's why Elizabeth had been so upset yesterday. This guy had two gears. One second he was Mr. Earnest Poetical Professor, and the next . . .

His gaze left her face, traveling slowly down her body.

Jessica swallowed. She knew her smile must be slipping. *Finish this*, she ordered herself.

"I just wanted to ask . . . um . . . do you think it would be, well, improper for students and teachers to date?" Jessica asked. She raised an eyebrow and gave him a one-sided, sexy little smile.

"Oh, I don't know," he said. He seemed to draw back a little. "That would depend on the teacher and the student. If the student was as intelligent and mature as you—for example—I think such an arrangement would be perfectly appropriate."

He stopped and gave Jessica an amused smile. "Of course," he continued, "the professor—myself, for example—would have to watch his step with the other faculty members. They might not approve."

Jessica pumped up her smile again. "I guess you know who I'm talking about," she said shyly.

"For you, Elizabeth, I would take the risk. We couldn't see each other in public . . ."

Jessica watched with morbid fascination as he

walked around the desk and stood in front of her.

"But in private . . ." He let the sentence trail off, its unspoken meaning startlingly clear. Suddenly his body pinned her hard against the desk, and his hands were buried in her golden hair.

Bruce stopped at a clear pool under a splashing little waterfall to clean out the gash on his wrist. The cold water hurt his wrist, then numbed and soothed it. Bruce tried not to look at the wound too closely. It was infected—how badly, he didn't want to know.

His hands were shaking from fever. Last night in the forest had been rough. He'd been cold and terrified. The fear hadn't been focused—he'd been afraid of every creaking branch, of supernatural hands groping toward him out of the blackness. Most of all he'd been scared of himself, babbling like an idiot to have someone to talk to, completely alone in the wilderness.

He had to rest. Bruce propped himself against a rotting log and took a deep breath.

Forests of pine and icy-blue snowcapped peaks spread out before him as far as he could see. "I've got a long way to go," he muttered. "I probably haven't even hiked a mile today."

Bruce shivered and wrapped his arms around himself. "Or maybe I don't. If I'm this sick, I may not wake up again. I may die against this log and rot into a skeleton. That's what Lila's probably doing somewhere else in this forest."

A violent shiver ran through him.

He could feel himself falling asleep, or maybe into delirium. Fever roared through him like the avalanche.

He saw Lila.

Her face was bloody and motionless in the plane. She was dead. Bruce ran from her, overcome with horror, collapsing into the snow.

Then they were running in the beautiful meadow again, chasing each other and laughing under the wide, sunlit blue sky. Lila threw a handful of dry grass at him.

She was lighting the fire, tossing sticks into the blaze. Lila looked over at him. The flames leaped up, reflected in her eyes.

"You've got as many lives as a cat," he said.

Lila smiled. "I'll survive."

Survive . . . survive . . .

Bruce woke with a jolt. He could still see Lila's face. He sat up, rubbing his eyes.

The sun was directly overhead, blazing off the snow. He breathed deeply the fresh, cold scent of ice melting on the pines.

Lila's alive, he thought. *I'd know if she wasn't. I'd feel it.*

He wished more than he'd ever wished anything in his life that he could find her. The next-best thing would be to make it out of the mountains alive and send help to her.

His wrist throbbed. "Time for a reality check. Take off the bandage," he ordered himself. He ripped off the tattered, dirty strip of Lila's red party dress.

Bruce swallowed. The skin around the deep cut in his wrist was an angry, swollen red. The cut was oozing yellow. He decided to leave it open, hoping that the fresh air would help it.

He got up and started through the forest. His steps were a little shaky, but he kept going.

I'll survive too, he thought.

Celine dumped the white rose onto Elizabeth's desk, scattering a couple of petals. How she had ended up Elizabeth Wakefield's flower girl was beyond her. Celine would have been happy to rip the rose to pieces.

She tried to tie a short yellow rope around the flower, the way William had told her to. Celine felt like an idiot. She was also about to break a nail.

"Why can't William do his own dirty work?" she complained aloud. It felt good to talk when she wasn't supposed to in the chilly, nasty old library.

Celine sighed. William hadn't told her what he was up to under the roof, but she knew it was going to be even nastier than the rose and rope. She picked them up for one last try. If this didn't work, she just might substitute her own plan.

Now, what would really upset Elizabeth? A library book open on its face, breaking the spine. Elizabeth would wring her hands and worry to death over that.

Of course, she'd be terrified by this hoax of William's. It would be some reward if Celine got to wait around and watch while the Prim Princess screamed her fool head off when she saw the tormented rose. But William wouldn't even let Celine do that.

"He's not much fun," Celine grumbled. "Damn!" A thorn had pricked her. She dropped the rose. She should drop William while she was at it.

Celine's memory of their pleasant oceanfront evening was becoming tainted. That lovely evening out wasn't to be repeated tonight after all: William had glided up in his wheelchair and told her he had a date he couldn't break at the institution tonight. Ha, ha. Did she really want to be seeing a guy who had to check into the insane asylum every night?

Celine rubbed her temples. That wasn't the only problem with this relationship. The more she thought about it, the more Elizabeth Wakefield seemed to be a constant presence in William's mind. Elizabeth's memory wasn't fading. If anything, it was getting stronger.

"He better not just be using me to get closer to Elizabeth," she said aloud.

Celine gave the rope a final twist and dropped the rose onto Elizabeth's desk.

"If I find out that's all he's doing, I may turn him in myself," she said to the rose.

Elizabeth slammed down the pay phone in the library landing. "The colossal jerks," she muttered. "Idiots! 'We can't release that information—it's confidential,'" she mimicked the security clerk she'd just spoken with.

Now what? "I'm down to my last half hour before Jessica has to report to security," she said to herself. "I need to get that sorority in trouble *right now.*"

Elizabeth walked slowly back to the stacks. Maybe if she went over to the security office, she could accomplish more in person. Why should the phone records be confidential? She probably had a right to see them. Or she could pretend she was doing a story for the TV station. . . .

As Elizabeth reached the door to the stacks, the elevator opposite the landing whisked open. Elizabeth saw somebody's back and a headful of honey-blond hair get into it. The elevator door closed.

Celine? Elizabeth thought. *Celine has never been in the library—I don't think she even knows how to read. Now, what's going on?*

Elizabeth walked between the bookshelves back to her carrel. *I'm not alone.* The thought sprang into her mind. She heard a soft *tick*—like the sound of a wheelchair rolling just a little. Elizabeth felt the back of her neck tingle.

Then she saw her desk and gasped. She covered her mouth to stifle a scream.

Her missing silk scarf lay on her desk; it was tied in a noose. The noose was strangling a white rose.

The shadows in the stacks seemed to leap wildly around her. Frantically Elizabeth tried to pick loose the knot in the scarf and free the rose. But it was no use—someone's hands had pulled and pulled the knot until it would never come undone. . . .

Elizabeth put a hand to her throat. It felt tight, as if the noose were already around it.

"Now you feel it," William whispered. He watched Elizabeth run wildly out of the room, dropping the scarf and some of her papers as she scrabbled at the door and slammed out.

William rolled his wheelchair over to reclaim the scarf. "Terror," he whispered, touching the scarf to his cheek. "We've played with parables, similes, and metaphors, Elizabeth. Now art will become life."

He and Elizabeth were way past the little notes and anonymous phone calls he'd managed last semester. Those antics had been fun, but they'd left something to be desired. Elizabeth had been briefly shaken up by the notes, William supposed, but he hadn't even been around to see it. He'd heard the fright in her voice when he'd called her at home over the Christmas vacation. That had been gratifying. But now . . . he wanted to go on to the next step.

William liked hangings. Especially if they were well-done. He had planned a whole series of hanging themes for Elizabeth's benefit. The rose strangled by the scarf was just the first.

"I'll find out what emotions you have," he told the scarf. "And just how strong they are. How you react to a good hanging will show me."

Celine had tried to talk him out of the rose the entire drive back from the diner to the campus. "It's a dead giveaway," she had said. "Who else but you would strangle a white rose?"

You would, William thought, smiling. The smile didn't reach his eyes. *You're a jealous cat.* It would be useful. All he had to do with Celine was wine and dine her, and perhaps occasionally spend the night, and she would help him with all his plans.

William felt a sudden qualm. What if Elizabeth found out and misunderstood?

"Those women don't mean anything, Elizabeth," he whispered. "Only you."

Celine was so stupid. She thought she could win him over with her tacky hair and obvious clothes.

"She's not like Elizabeth," William said softly.

Was anyone? He'd spent hours, lying on his back in the madhouse and smoking, thinking exactly what Elizabeth was like. She was perfect. Her drive to discover beauty and truth, her classic good looks, the smoldering passion that the right man could fan into flames. William almost laughed aloud. Kissing her was like reading a poem, with all the delicious physical feelings thrown in.

How had he lived all these months without kissing her? William put his lips to the scarf. "Kissing won't be enough now," he said softly. He wanted her to be his all night. Where? Well, he had one idea about that. William laughed and jingled the key to Elizabeth's Jeep, which he had just stolen out of her knapsack.

William stroked the rose. Then he easily untied the knot in the noose. And tied it again. "This is what I'll do with you," he said softly. "Tie you up for a bit. Let you go. Maybe strangle you. Maybe not."

William was amazed at the precision of his genius. By the time he revealed himself to Elizabeth, she would be begging for mercy. "And then the jaws will gently close," William whispered, stroking his face with the scarf.

Jessica desperately twisted her head away from Professor Martin's urgently seeking lips. He was pressing her into the desk so hard she could scarcely breathe.

Don't panic! Jessica screamed to herself.

Professor Martin tried to pull her face to his. "You are so sexy," he said with a groan. "I want to know you better—oh, a lot better, Elizabeth. The two of us together will be the stuff of which dreams are made."

Jessica shoved him aside. He made a grab for her. She dodged, slamming her backpack sideways into the desk, and raced to the door. *I hope the tape recorder didn't get smacked to pieces,* Jessica thought. "You're nailed, you creep," she said, laughing triumphantly. "Hold it right there."

Professor Martin smiled. He took a step toward her.

Not taking her eyes off him, Jessica opened her backpack and pulled out the still-functioning tape recorder. "Now you listen to me," she said. "Either you drop those charges against me for stealing your precious book, or I play this tape over the campus loudspeakers."

Chapter Fourteen

"So I heard you've been having a little excitement around here," Elizabeth said casually to the clerk at the security office. She had forced her attention from murdered white roses to the more pressing matter at hand. She'd get Celine for the rose trick later.

The clerk seemed taken aback for a moment. Then he smirked. "Yeah, your look-alike has been gracing the corridors."

Elizabeth didn't know this guy, but he was almost definitely a student. He was the right age. He had a short military haircut and wore a beige uniform shirt.

Elizabeth smiled, a dimple appearing in her left cheek. "What's your name?"

"Jeffrey." The guy just stood there and waited. Elizabeth wasn't sure if he was being difficult or if he was just dumb.

"I need a little information," she said.

The guy smiled, but his expression was condescending. "*Maybe* I can help you. Most of what we do here is confidential."

Does he think he works for the CIA? Elizabeth thought. "Didn't I just talk to you over the phone?" she asked.

"Guess so."

She realized that she should have developed a concrete strategy before coming here. Elizabeth doubted if a straightforward approach to get what she needed would work now, but she might as well try.

"I'd like to see your phone log for last Tuesday night," she said.

"I just told you on the phone you couldn't."

"You told me you couldn't give that information over the phone," Elizabeth said, exasperated.

"I didn't say you could get it in person, either." Jeffrey looked pleased with himself.

"May I see the log?" Elizabeth asked, using up her last shred of politeness. For all she knew, while this dialogue was going on, Jessica was being led to prison in handcuffs.

"Why?" the guy countered.

"Do I really have to explain to you?" Elizabeth asked. "Aren't I just allowed to see it?"

"I don't think so." Jeffrey looked uncertain. "My boss isn't here right now."

Aha. Opportunity. "Well, I think your boss

would let me see it." Elizabeth looked Jeffrey in the eyes and turned a megawatt smile on him. "I'm doing a report for WSVU, the campus television station, on efficiency in the security office. I know a call was placed to security on Tuesday night, and I just want to make sure it was logged correctly."

"Of course it was," Jeffrey said belligerently. "I was on duty last Tuesday night."

"Let's see." Elizabeth held out her hand.

Jeffrey hesitated.

"Then I'll interview you," Elizabeth said. "You'll be on TV."

Jeffrey reached under the counter and produced a black notebook. "I really shouldn't be doing this without authorization," he said.

"Your boss will be madder if you don't," Elizabeth assured him. "If he finds out you let slip an opportunity for some very favorable news coverage of the security office, he'll have your head on a platter."

"I guess so." Jeffrey didn't look completely convinced.

Elizabeth opened the book. She half expected him to snatch it away, but he didn't. Good, each page was dated. Elizabeth quickly flipped to Tuesday.

Nothing. Elizabeth's mouth dropped open. She had been so sure she could clear Jessica by finding the record of that call. Now what? Jeffrey had said he couldn't have made a mistake in logging it. Elizabeth's heart sank to her shoes.

"If you're looking for the call that was made to set up your sister, that was on Monday," Jeffrey said.

He wasn't stupid, after all. Elizabeth looked at him gratefully. *That makes sense. If the call hadn't been made in advance, the security officers might have been out yelling at people to turn down their stereos instead of on hand to trap Jessica.* Someone had really been thinking there. But why had security sent enough troops to take Baghdad after Jessica?

Elizabeth wondered how far she could push Jeffrey to help her. She leaned across the counter a little. "You took the call?"

"Yeah."

"Who was it?" This was the million-dollar question. Elizabeth held her breath.

"They didn't say." Jeffrey shrugged. "They usually don't. But it was a woman. We have caller ID on our emergency line, and so I knew the call was coming from Theta House."

"You remember all this from four days ago?" Elizabeth cautiously flipped to Monday in the log.

"You would too, after what happened. I mean, that was the most excitement we've had since I've been working here. We spent most of Monday getting everything in place for the arrest."

"Security did all that to nab a sorority girl snitching a book?" Elizabeth said incredulously.

"That wasn't the crime the caller reported." Jeffrey looked embarrassed. "We sort of made a mistake. Hey, this is off the record, OK? Or report this saying that security goes to extreme measures to protect the lives of SVU students."

"I'll represent everything in an extremely positive light," Elizabeth said. She was so impatient by this time that she wanted to shake the words out of him. "What crime did you think my sister was going to commit?"

"We didn't think it was an SVU student at all," Jeffrey said. "The caller said the person who would be in the professor's office was a career criminal who'd just escaped from prison. We'd read in the paper last week that somebody like that *was* at large."

Elizabeth glanced at the log. There it was, the number and date of the call.

"That's a private number over at Theta," Jeffrey added grudgingly.

Elizabeth smiled at him again. Jessica had a directory of the Thetas' phone numbers in their room. In ten minutes Elizabeth would know exactly who had called.

"May I have a copy of this, please?" She couldn't wait to have the evidence in her own hands.

Jeffrey copied the page and gave it to her. Elizabeth stuffed it into her backpack and rushed out the door.

"Hey, aren't you going to film me for the interview?" Jeffrey yelled after her.

"Yes, later—I'm going to recommend you for the Medal of Honor!" Elizabeth yelled, running backward along the path. *But first I have to find Jessica. What's she going to think of her so-called sisters now?*

"You're not Elizabeth," Professor Martin said, drawing a deep, gasping breath. He couldn't seem to believe it.

"That doesn't make any difference," Jessica said quickly.

He was moving toward her, very slowly.

"She feels the same way that I do about you," Jessica went on, backing out the doorway. "That's another condition I've got: You stop bothering my sister in any way. If you do that, and call campus security this instant and tell them you're dropping the charges against me, I'll destroy this tape," Jessica said rapidly. "If you don't, I'll make absolutely sure everyone on campus knows what you tried on me. I don't think you'll have a job then."

Maybe she had gone too far. Professor Martin's face darkened with anger.

"Give me the tape!" he hissed.

Jessica backed into the hall, her heart in her throat. "Not until you do what I want." What would happen now? It was a standoff.

Professor Martin looked at her, then at the

phone on his desk. Suddenly he lunged at her.

Jessica barely avoided his groping hands. She turned and ran. *I can't let him get the tape!* she thought as she raced down the hall. *Then it will just be my word against his. And they'll take his word. No one's going to believe me about anything now, when I'm in so much trouble.*

She could hear Professor Martin's feet thundering behind her. He was bigger and faster than she was. Would she make it to the outside door before he caught her?

"Jessica?"

Professor Taschek, her chemistry teacher, was looking around the outside doorway. Jessica had never been so relieved to see anyone.

"Is something wrong?" he asked.

Jessica looked behind her. The sound of charging feet had stopped. Professor Martin was gasping and panting. He had his hands in his pants pockets and was sauntering toward her down the hall.

"No, we've just been reading Byron," he said. The anger had evaporated from his face, but it was still flushed.

Professor Taschek frowned. Jessica wondered if he'd seen them tearing down the hall.

Professor Martin glared back. "What are you doing in the humanities building?" he snapped.

"Looking for the faculty meeting." Professor Taschek glanced behind him. Jessica heard voices.

Thank God, she said to herself. *People. I hope the whole faculty is out there.*

"The meeting was two days ago," Professor Martin said coldly.

"I guess I missed it, then. I really am an absent-minded professor," Professor Taschek said with his kindly smile.

Jessica looked out through the open door and saw that Professor Taschek was leading a whole herd of lost chemistry professors.

"I'll walk back to the chemistry building with you if you don't mind," she said. "I didn't quite understand the discussion in class this morning of the Bohr atom." At the time Jessica had thought of it as the Boring atom, but now nothing interested her more.

"I'd be happy to explain it to you again," Professor Taschek said.

Jessica stepped through the outside door with him and looked back. "Don't forget the call you need to make," she said to Professor Martin. She patted her backpack.

Professor Martin stared at her. His face was twisted with rage.

"Wait till Jessica hears about Alison," Elizabeth said to Tom. "I couldn't find her anywhere, but she's supposed to meet me here at the room before she goes to security. Maybe she'll finally be ready to dump the Thetas for good after I tell her what they tried to do to her." Elizabeth drew a shuddering breath. Then she got up from her desk chair and walked over to the window. The gloomy rain outside matched her mood.

"Elizabeth?" Tom stood behind her. His warm hands dropped onto her shoulders. "What's the matter?" he asked softly.

Elizabeth's shoulders drooped. "I'm miserable."

"Why?" Tom asked, gently massaging her. "You've been under a lot of pressure lately, but it looks like that's going to ease up now."

"Oh, that's not it. I'm upset about something else. I didn't want to tell you what happened yesterday, but I really should." Elizabeth faced him. Her blue-green eyes were deeply troubled. "I had a problem with Professor Martin."

"What kind of a problem?" Tom asked. He could feel his heart rate speed up.

"You have to promise not to get mad."

"I don't promise at all. My gut is telling me I know what you're going to say." Tom balled his fists.

"Good." Elizabeth turned back to the window. "Because I don't want to say it."

Tom turned her around again. "Tell me, Elizabeth. Please. It's important."

"Well . . ." Elizabeth hesitated.

"Don't leave anything out," Tom ordered. He took her hands. "Tell me exactly what happened." She was really scaring him.

"I shouldn't let this get to me the way it has." Elizabeth shook her head. "He didn't really even do anything. He just *tried* to . . ."

"Tried to what?" Tom kept his voice calm. She might not tell him the rest if she thought it would make him angry. His heart banged furiously.

"He tried to kiss me in his office, and he was rubbing my arm," Elizabeth said. She flushed. "I know that sounds like nothing. But I felt threatened—I didn't know if he would stop."

Tom was speechless.

"Will I look like a baby if I report him?" she asked. "I don't even know if it's against the school rules to do what he did. So he touched my arm and cheek. Big deal, right?"

"That's completely bogus, Liz." Tom drew a deep breath. Then he slammed his fist into the door. "That stinking, no-good slime. If he ever touches you again, or *thinks* about touching you again, he's not going to know what hit him."

"Oh, Tom." Elizabeth was blinking back tears. She pulled out of his arms and walked to the other side of the room. "I'm so embarrassed about this. I should have seen what was coming—I'm not fourteen years old. But I didn't want to. That's the worst part," she said, looking away.

"Of course you didn't think he would try something like that." Tom tried to speak calmly through the raging in his brain. Right now Elizabeth needed him to listen and help her make sense out of what had happened, not go out and murder the professor. He could do that later. "Working with Martin sounded like a great opportunity at first," he said, as reasonably as he could. "So you gave him credit for being better than he was. That's nothing to be ashamed about."

She still looked so forlorn. Tom walked over and took her in his arms. "We'll figure out what to do," he whispered, cupping her face in his hands.

"I love you," Elizabeth sobbed. "And I don't deserve you."

"Because of what happened? Just because he touched you? Are you crazy?" Tom drew back to look at her in amazement. Even when her eyes were filled with tears and her face twisted with pain, she was beautiful. So very beautiful.

"No, not because of that. Well, sort of because of that." Elizabeth remembered the silly daydreams she'd had about Professor Martin. She rubbed her face against Tom's shirt. "I—I can't explain. But I'm just so glad you're here."

"Me too," Tom said, cradling her in his arms. He wanted to kiss away her hurt, to feel his lips on hers and her satin skin under his hands.

After what had happened with Martin, though, she might not like it. "Is this OK?" he asked softly, running his fingertips across her back.

Elizabeth leaned into his embrace. "It's wonderful," she whispered. Her hands reached up for his face, stroking it, then ran luxuriously through his dark hair. Their mouths met in a deep kiss.

Jessica opened the door and looked cautiously around it. "Am I interrupting something?"

"I just saw Professor Martin," Jessica said breezily, dropping her purse onto the bed and combing her fingers through her rain-soaked hair. "He doesn't send his regards."

Tom and Elizabeth sat side by side on Elizabeth's bed. They looked like two of the black storm clouds that were hanging over the campus.

"Cheer up, you guys," Jessica said. "Professor Martin has changed his mind. He's dropping all the charges against me."

"What!" Elizabeth stared at her in astonishment. "How? Just yesterday he told me he could never do that because it was against his principles!"

"Well, he has a new set of principles today." Jessica plugged in the blow dryer. How was she going to explain to Elizabeth what she'd done? Elizabeth had a tendency to get upset when Jessica impersonated her.

She might not have to know, Jessica thought, switching on the dryer and letting the warm stream lift her silky hair.

"I'm curious how you turned the situation around," Tom said loudly over the noise of the dryer. He got up and stood behind Jessica.

Jessica switched off the dryer and moved away.

She'd had enough of male contact for the afternoon. "You don't want to know the dirty details, believe me." Jessica stared at herself in the mirror. She felt like washing her hair with detergent to get Professor Martin's touch out of it. A lot of scalding hot water would feel good on the rest of her too. And mouthwash. Yuck.

"Yes, I do." Elizabeth had a funny look on her face. "I mean, this is wonderful, Jessica. An hour ago you were headed for the penitentiary, and now everyone is willing to forgive and forget. . . . What *did* you say to Professor Martin? He wouldn't let you off even for me. . . ."

Elizabeth blushed violently.

Tom scowled. He got up and strode around the room, rumpling his hair.

Jessica looked from one to the other. *Liz told him,* she realized.

Elizabeth was looking at Jessica's clothes—*her* clothes—as if she were trying to recognize them.

"I really don't see why we have to get into it," Jessica said quickly. "Let's just drop the subject. I think we all know Professor Martin, and what happened in his office wasn't pleasant."

"How pleasant wasn't it?" Tom asked coldly.

He sat back on the bed with Elizabeth. They waited, staring at her.

"Who cares?" Jessica said, exasperated. "The charges are dropped. Professor Martin won't bother you anymore, Liz. And I'm going to be a

Theta. I think that after everything that's happened, no one is going to be able to say I'm not loyal to the house."

"Why are you wearing my clothes?" Elizabeth asked abruptly, getting up and walking over to her. Elizabeth really looked bad, Jessica realized with a pang: She'd been crying, and she had circles under her eyes. Tom looked like a homicidal maniac.

"I couldn't find a thing that was clean," Jessica said lightly.

Elizabeth was staring at her. "Oh, no. You pretended to be me again. Jessica, you shouldn't have gone anywhere near Professor Martin. What if he'd . . ."

Jessica saw understanding dawn in her sister's eyes. "He did jump you," Elizabeth finished. "And for some insane reason, you planned it."

"Liz, it wasn't insane—it worked." Jessica drew a shaky breath. She wondered how long she would keep remembering the scenes from that office.

"Tell us exactly what happened." Elizabeth was boring in on her with a look.

"I think you know. I don't want to upset you with the details." Jessica turned back to the mirror and fanned her hair with the blow dryer again.

"I'm upset already!" Elizabeth yelled.

Jessica switched off the dryer again and looked at herself in the mirror with a martyred expression. At this rate she would catch pneumonia before she got her hair dry.

"Jessica, you probably should talk about what happened," Tom said quietly. "I know what he tried on Elizabeth. If it was the same thing . . ."

"If I'm going to take legal action against Professor Martin, I need to know what else he's done," Elizabeth said, her voice fierce.

Jessica frowned. Elizabeth wasn't going to like this at all. It would be better for her if she dropped the whole thing. But Elizabeth never let anything drop. It must be her reporter instincts.

Jessica faced them. "All right. I went to Martin's office pretending to be you, Elizabeth. He fell for it completely. Then I asked him if he thought we could date."

Elizabeth made a choking noise. "That was supposed to be *me* saying that."

"Well, don't worry—he doesn't think you mean it anymore."

"Go on, Jessica." Tom's dark eyes were intent.

Jessica looked away. This was the bad part. "He said we couldn't date, at least in public, because it would ruin his reputation. Then he . . . did some awful things, with my hair and my clothes, before I shoved him off." Jessica's hands were shaking a little. Now that the danger was past, her adrenaline must be wearing off.

"This is outrageous!" Elizabeth shouted, leaping up. "Jessica, I'm not waiting any longer to report him. We're going back to security right now!"

Jessica sagged onto her desk. "Liz, please. I've seen enough of security for a while. And I'm sure they've seen enough of me. Besides, we need to think about this. I told Professor Martin I wouldn't report him."

"Are you going to keep your word?" Tom asked tightly.

Jessica frowned. "I don't know. Right after I left him, I called security and found out that he really did drop the charges. He told them that since he got back his prized book, pressing the charges wasn't really worth the trouble. So Martin kept his end of the bargain." Jessica paused. "But I didn't erase the tape."

"What tape?" Tom looked surprised.

"The tape I made of our whole conversation."

"Jessica, you're wonderful!" Elizabeth said excitedly. "Where is it?"

Jessica opened her backpack and produced a plastic sandwich bag with the tape inside it.

"Mind if I hear a little of it?" Tom asked.

Jessica looked at her sister. Elizabeth was going to bounce off the walls when she heard the tape—and not because Jessica had impersonated her.

"I don't think that's a good idea," she said. Why was Tom putting them through this? Jessica didn't want to hear the tape either.

"I do," Elizabeth said firmly. "It'll be real proof that he harasses students."

Jessica shook her head and pushed PLAY on the

little recorder. She set it on her desk. "You can ask me anything, Elizabeth. . . ." came Professor Martin's voice.

"He sounds like somebody on a soap opera," Jessica said. Tom and Elizabeth didn't smile.

"I've wanted to do this all semester. . . ."

Jessica hit FORWARD.

"I'm glad we understand each other now. . . ."

Elizabeth slammed the STOP button on the recorder. She looked as if someone had knocked the wind out of her. Her cheeks were flushed, and her blue-green eyes snapped sparks.

"That dirtbag!" she raged. "The administration is going to hear about this!"

"Hear about what, Elizabeth?" Tom said, very quietly. "Jessica came on to him. And she's not a minor. What he did isn't criminal. Touching your cheek and making you feel the way he did is probably harassment, but it's going to be hard to prove."

Elizabeth's mouth dropped open. "He can't just get away with this!"

"Oh, he won't." Jessica removed the tape from the player. "I've still got ammunition as long as I have this. He doesn't want anyone to know what happened, believe me."

Tom held out his hand. "Let me take care of that tape."

"Why?"

"We should copy it and put both copies in different, safe places," he said.

Jessica frowned. "I don't know what the big deal is now that he isn't pressing charges," she said. "I was just going to stick it in a drawer."

"That tape is a very big deal," Tom said.

"Blackmail." Elizabeth nodded. She seemed to have calmed down a little.

"I did tell him I'd erase it," Jessica said. "But I thought I'd keep it and see if he behaves himself around female students. I kind of think that after this he will, at least for a while."

"Even if you do erase the tape, Martin will think you still have it." Tom shook his head. "You'll be dealing with a desperate man, Jessica. As long as you have that tape, you could ruin his career, his whole life. It might be very dangerous for you to leave it lying around."

"All right, take it. I certainly don't want it around." Jessica shrugged. "Thanks, Tom."

"I still want to call back the lawyer I consulted about the book fiasco and tell him about Professor Martin," Elizabeth said angrily.

"Liz, stop making such a major issue out of it." Jessica sighed. "I know he's a creep, but at least the robbery business is over. Unless the Thetas still have an excuse to keep me out, this saga is over."

Elizabeth wrinkled her forehead. "Alison Quinn hates you, Jessica. I have a feeling your troubles with that girl are just beginning."

Chapter Fifteen

"I'm ready to go," Mrs. Winkler announced, zipping up her suitcase. "You two can have your bedroom back."

Billie hugged her mother. "We didn't mind letting you use it. Mom—how long have you known it was 'our' bedroom?"

"Oh, since the first time Steven answered the phone," Mrs. Winkler said. "He didn't exactly sound like a guest. But I also knew just by the way Billie talked about you, Steven."

"What did she say?" Steven asked, feeling shy.

"It wasn't so much what she said as how she said it." Billie's mother smiled. "I could tell that she loves you. And when you love someone, you want to be with that person day and night."

Mr. Winkler appeared in the doorway. "Let's go," he said. "We've got a three-hour drive ahead of us."

"When did you first figure out Billie's little secret?" Mrs. Winkler asked him, picking up her suitcase and following Mr. Winkler to the door of the apartment.

"I bet I know," Steven said sheepishly. "It was when I banged on the ceiling that night."

Mr. Winkler looked surprised. "I had no idea that was you, or even a human being. I banged back the next night to keep up the ritual. I didn't want to worry the spooks."

"Oh, Dad." Billie grabbed his arm. "Don't tease Steven."

Mr. Winkler grinned and opened the door. He drew Billie to him for a quick kiss on the cheek. "Take care, Steven. Watch out for things that go bump in the night."

"Liz, are you trying to make me paranoid? Your voice sounds so ominous!" Jessica waited for an explanation.

"I just got back from doing a little research at the security office, Jess." Elizabeth shook her head. "And I found out that you were definitely set up. Security was tipped off about exactly where you would be and at what time. Not only that, the call came from Theta House. So who called?" Elizabeth asked rhetorically.

"So that's what happened," Jessica murmured.

"I happen to know who called," Elizabeth said.

"Alison, right? I just hope none of the other

Thetas are out to get me too." Jessica picked up her brush. This was horrible news. She wished Elizabeth would stop badgering her and give her time to digest it.

"Who else do you think is in on this besides Alison? Think," Elizabeth commanded.

"Liz, I can't think anymore right now." Jessica grabbed her towel from the rack on the closet. She was ready for that hot shower. "Why do we have to settle everything today? Do you have a press deadline?"

"I shudder to think what Alison might do next," Elizabeth said grimly.

"She's wanted me out of her way since I got her order wrong when I was waitressing at the coffeehouse." Jessica shrugged. "The more I try to avoid her, the more she hates me."

"Alison sounds obsessed," Tom said thoughtfully.

"She doesn't have any reason to be. She's vice president of the Thetas; I'm a freshman-pledge nobody." Jessica frowned. "The only reason I can think of for Alison to set me up is that she had nothing else to do for fun."

"Jessica, this was never meant to be funny." Elizabeth frowned. "When Alison made that call, she knew all along that—"

"I could be expelled from school," Jessica finished. "Listen, I'm sure you're right that Alison set me up. And I'll get back at her."

"Jessica—" Elizabeth tried to interrupt.

"I'll hit her where it really hurts." Jessica gathered her shampoo, soap, and cream rinse and headed for the door. "I want to think up something really special for her. No matter how long it takes. She's going to be sorry she did this."

Tom and Elizabeth were silent. When Jessica finally looked over at them, she saw their faces were troubled.

Jessica let out a bitter laugh. "When Alison sees the plot I'm going to come up with to crush her, she's going to wish she never heard of Lord Byron."

"Please come with me to the BSU meeting," Nina begged Elizabeth. She leaned over the table they were sharing at lunch. "You're my test case. I want to see if Bryan really meant what he said about respecting my ideological differences. If he does, it should be all right that you're at the meeting and he should let you march with us against racism. If not, I'll know he just thinks of me as a pretty face."

Elizabeth looked at her intently. "In other words, if you don't get your way, you're going to break up with him?"

"I don't know." Nina could feel herself starting to blush. "I mean, we *already* broke up. But if he shows me that we're not as different as we seem, and that he'll listen to my opinions, who knows what could happen?"

Elizabeth made a face and bit into a radish. "I don't know, Nina. After everything that's been happening with Jessica and Professor Martin, all I need is a little more stress. I'm going to feel awfully uncomfortable at your meeting. What if Bryan orders me out of there?"

"Then we'll leave together," Nina said resolutely. "Come on, Elizabeth. How else can I do this?"

Elizabeth sighed. "All right. I believe that I should march against racism. It makes sense that I go to the meeting about it."

Elizabeth didn't have her phobia about marching in public with a picket sign, Nina realized. "You'll make a better BSU member than I do," she said. "Come on. The meeting's already started. I have a feeling we're going to make a dramatic entrance."

Elizabeth stuck her fork upright in her salad. "Let's go," she said. "Before I lose my nerve."

"Don't worry too much," Nina told her friend as they hurried across the quad to the social-science building. "I think only a few people are really against the idea of your marching. Everybody else is just listening to Bryan. He's right about a lot of things, so they trust him."

The meeting room was full. Nina saw several black people she didn't recognize; they were probably students from other colleges. Elizabeth really stuck out, especially since all the chairs were taken. She and Elizabeth had to stand in full view by the door.

Bryan was sitting on the other side of the table. He frowned when he saw them. Nina wasn't sure if it was a thoughtful frown or an I'm-going-to-get-you-for-this frown.

"Elizabeth is interested in our cause," Nina announced, trying to keep her voice from shaking. Might as well take the bull by the horns and tell everyone what they were doing there. Then it would be over with, whatever happened.

"Welcome, Elizabeth," said Rosa, nodding.

"I'd like very much to march with you," Elizabeth said firmly, turning to everyone in the room.

"It'll dilute the message if white people march with us," Tony Ellis said. He didn't look at Elizabeth or Nina. "In the sixties we needed those people," he said to Bryan. "Now we can go on by ourselves."

"Go on where?" Bryan asked.

"To fully equal rights," Tony said.

"Why is that just a black thing?" Nina asked in exasperation.

"It's not," Elizabeth said. "It's everybody's concern."

Nina looked at Bryan. He was twirling a pencil around his fingers. *He's not going to support us,* she thought desperately. *This is horrible. He and I are finished as a couple.*

Bryan slowly stood. He looked at Nina, then at Elizabeth.

"I think . . ."

Nina gulped.

"That the march should be open to everybody," Bryan said. He held up a hand as Tony started to interrupt. "There are some practical reasons for that—after all, there's strength in numbers." Bryan smiled at Nina. "But the real reason is that anybody who's against racism should be encouraged to take a stand. I know that's not what I've been saying, but I was wrong."

Nina sagged against the wall as relief washed over her. Elizabeth squeezed her hand.

"All in favor?" Bryan asked the members. Everybody's hand went up except Tony's. Finally, slowly, he raised his hand too.

"It's unanimous," Bryan said. "OK, let's get out of here, everybody. We'll set up a meeting next week to make signs and finalize the plan for the march."

Elizabeth and Nina walked out of the social-science building together. "Thanks," Elizabeth said.

"Thank *you*," Nina said sincerely. "I won't forget this, Elizabeth. You're the best friend I ever had."

"Except maybe for one person." Elizabeth

tilted her head to the left. "Here comes Bryan. I'll see you later."

Bryan walked over to Nina, whistling.

He'd better not think he's done me a favor, Nina thought. She'd been right about the march. "You look happy," she said.

"I am." Bryan took her hand and led her to the low stone wall in front of the building. He sat her down. "Let's settle some things," he said. "I may be a little stubborn, but I do listen carefully to everything you say—it just takes me a little while to let it sink in. And I don't just want to date you because you're pretty. "

"But you do think I'm pretty, don't you?" Nina asked, grinning.

"Beautiful," Bryan said. His mouth met hers in a long, exquisite kiss.

"Are we all made up?" Nina asked when they finally drew back.

"Of course we are. We'll lead the march together." Bryan kissed her again. "You can carry the biggest sign."

Chapter Sixteen

"I'd very much like another muffin," Lila said to an imaginary Alison Quinn, sweeping a pine branch out of her way. "Could you pass the orange marmalade, Kimberly?"

"I'd be delighted to, Lila," Kimberly said. "After lunch we're going shopping. Why don't you join us?"

"I'd like to more than anything," Lila said fervently, jumping over a log. That was the truth.

She turned and looked behind her. The small plane was still visible in the distance.

She had to keep her mind on other things besides her exhaustion and terror. She was beginning to wonder how long her sanity would hold out. If only Tisiano were there, he would protect her from this hell. *Of course, if Tisiano were alive, I wouldn't even be here—I wouldn't even be in the United States.*

"Jess, are you coming shopping?" she asked a small gray-and-white bird perched in a tree. "We'll keep each other company while we hunt for bargains."

Bruce might not be much of a bargain, but Lila wished he were there. As for hunting . . . she'd thought she'd seen shadows just beyond the firelight, big shapes. . . . It was almost night. What should she go shopping for?

"Shoes," Lila mumbled, looking over her shoulder. "A pair of Italian shoes, with at least two-inch heels, very spare and classy."

A bush crackled. Every time she moved, something seemed to move behind her. She hadn't yet seen the wolves. But they were there. Lila's heart pounded.

"What, Alison?" Lila asked over the roaring in her ears. "A fur coat would be nice for this weather? If I had a club, I could make you one." *If only I had a weapon.*

The sun's last slanting rays vanished. Nightfall.

Lila saw a low cliff up ahead. She could build a fire in front of it and . . . try to live through another night.

The solitary cry of a wolf rang out.

"So what did you have to tell me that's so urgent we couldn't even relax over our salads at dinner first?" Elizabeth joked. "This better be good, Nina."

"It's not." Nina's voice was grave. "I think you'd better sit down to hear it."

Elizabeth let her friend steer her to a bench just off the path back to their dorm. Elizabeth grimaced as a pool of water on the bench promptly soaked through the seat of her jeans. The storm that afternoon had thoroughly watered the campus.

Elizabeth opened her mouth to ask Nina if she had lost her mind or if she just liked sopping, clammy clothes. But Nina had her face in her hands. She didn't seem to notice the wet bench or the rain misting out of the overhanging trees, dripping from her colorfully braided hair.

Elizabeth had never seen Nina so grim. A slight tremor of foreboding ran through her.

Nina looked into Elizabeth's eyes. "Elizabeth, all that weird stuff you told me about what's been going on with you in the library—the strangled rose, shadows almost turning into people—somebody really hates you."

"Celine, of course," Elizabeth said quickly. "She's been out to get me for weeks. And I saw her leaving the library right after I found the rose."

Nina shook her head. "She may be part of it, but something much worse is going on, Elizabeth."

Elizabeth forced her voice to stay calm. Nina wasn't prone to panic. She would look this frightened only about something absolutely terrible. "How do you know?" she asked. "What happened?"

"Bryan stopped by my room this afternoon after the BSU meeting, and of course that was the end of getting any work done." Nina almost smiled, but the smile didn't quite make it to her lips. "So finally I went to the library to study. About an hour ago I was up on the top floor again, where the legal documents are. I heard somebody come in. I thought it might be you—you're the only person who knows I go up there. But—"

"Celine?" Elizabeth asked. Her hands were shaking.

Nina sighed heavily. "No. I heard this person creeping around, and I thought it might be a prowler. So I got up as quietly as I could and tiptoed around the edge of the room to the door. My books are still up there—I just left them."

Nina's lips were trembling. "I still wasn't sure anything was wrong—I just had this awful feeling. Then I saw . . . *it* back in a corner. Your aqua scarf. Two dolls were bound together with string like they were kissing or something, and your scarf was . . . *hanging* them from one of the bookshelves. And a big, thick rope was coming from a hook on the ceiling. Oh, Elizabeth, it was tied in a *real* noose. I was so scared, I couldn't even scream. I mean, I was in the middle of a crazy house—the library had suddenly been turned into a hanging gallery. . . ."

Elizabeth's stomach lurched. That wasn't something Celine would do. Celine might be spiteful, but she wasn't a killer. Who, then? The rose pointed to William White. But William was safely locked up in a mental institution.

"I'd like to believe it's someone's idea of a sick joke, but . . ." Nina's voice trailed off. Elizabeth felt Nina's whole body shaking next to her. When her friend spoke again, Elizabeth could hardly hear her.

"I think I barely made it out of there alive. But, Elizabeth . . . I was just there by accident. You've got to be careful. That whole show . . ."

"I know," Elizabeth said flatly. "It was for me."

***Jessica thinks James Montgomery is almost perfect—he's got looks, brains, and plenty of charisma. Find out what happens when Jessica and James get closer, in Sweet Valley University #10*, NO MEANS NO.**